PRAGUE

Adrian Wheeler

Adrian Wheeler

PRAGUE CONSPIRACY

Imprint

This edition first published in 2024 by Adrian Wheeler and Company Limited

Copyright © Adrian Wheeler 2024

The right of Adrian Wheeler to be identified as the Author of the Work has been asserted by him in accordance with the Copyright, Designs and Patents Act 1988

All rights reserved
All characters in this publication are fictitious and any resemblance to real persons, living or dead, is purely coincidental

KPD ISBN 9798336342598
Manufacture: Amazon Distribution

Independently published by
Adrian Wheeler and Company Limited
The Old Rectory
Church Street
Weybridge KT13 8DE
United Kingdom

Cover design: Dr C W R Priebe
Cover photo: Thomas Wheeler
The work including its parts is protected by copyright. Any use without the consent of the author/publisher is not permitted. This applies in particular to electronic or other reproduction, translation, distribution and making publicly available.

Dedication

This book is dedicated to my family, who brought me to Prague.

I would like to thank Dr C W R Priebe for his generous advice and help from start to finish.

Table of Contents

Dedication I
Table of Contents II
A Meeting with Fabian 1
The Church of The Holy Nativity 7
A Day at Work 10
Licence to Kill 16
Andrew Lloyd 21
My New Colleagues 25
The Golden Lion 28
Barrandov 33
Cassandra 37
Pad Thai 45
Dragunov 48
Operation *Can Has* 54
A Phone-call to William 57
Cloak and Dagger 60
Carsten 64
Andelsky Pivovar 70
The Vernissage 75
My Clever Idea 78
Not a Welder 81
A Second Opinion 86
Katerina 90
Andrew. I Make a Mistake 94
A Day at the Races 98
Good Dog 108
On the Road 111
Tabor 117
Cold Water 123

Table of Contents

The Journey Home 127
Back to Work 130
A Demonstration 133
The Review 136
An Invitation 139
Major Butterworth 142
A Message from Aunt Jemima 147
Domestic Bliss 150
A Visitor 153
The Appliance of Science 156
Her Story 162
A Drink with Alasdair 167
Andrew's Future 173
Petra's Lesson 175
Pencak Silat 180
A Dinner Invitation 184
Heroes 187
Galena's Preview 193
Face-to-Face with God 198
Andelska Hora 203
Trevor Toll 212
Sarka Valley 220
Unarmed Combat 224
Czech Glossary i

A Meeting with Fabian

When I went into the shop the sun was shining. When I came out it was snowing. 'Typical Prague weather. Roll on spring'. Then I remembered that spring in this country didn't mean daffodils. It meant Warsaw Pact tanks in the streets.

I was meeting Fabian, so I needed cigarettes. It was the end of January, and I thought I'd given up. I usually made it to March, and once April, but a meeting with Fabian meant Camel Yellow.

They'd been quiet all winter, which made me happy – like a toothache that suddenly isn't there any more. But they were *always* lurking in the background, silent for weeks then erupting with one of their peremptory calls to duty. This was a classic:

'Aunt Eleanor has been taken into hospital. Can you meet the family lawyer at 10 am next Tuesday to talk about her assets?'

'Aunt' meant Café Slavia on Narodn*í*. 'Eleanor' meant a single person from the Department. 'Assets' meant we would be talking about some kind of financial chicanery. 'Lawyer' meant that it would probably be semi-legal at best. All I needed to know.

I wandered along the Vltava embankment. It wasn't far. There was a chilly breeze coming off the river but the air was fresh and invigorating. As usual, I paused once or twice to look behind me at the 'Castle' – the sprawling fortress on a hill which has dominated Prague since the Middle Ages. Its stone walls change colour with the movement of the sun and clouds. I could watch this display for hours, and sometimes have. Tour parties going in the other direction blocked the

A Meeting with Fabian

pavement every fifty metres. I felt polite today, so I stepped into the road.

The Slavia wasn't crowded. The breakfast rush was over, so half the tables were empty. The others were occupied by a nondescript collection of *flaneurs*. I tried to imagine that they were all writers, actors, directors and musicians, as they would have been in Havel's day. But they were probably just businessmen like me. In one corner were four women talking animatedly. This was unusual. The normal haunt for 'ladies who lunch' was the Café Savoy on the other side of the bridge. I could faintly hear *'Ma Vlast'* beneath the buzz of conversation. This was the Slavia: patriotic name, patriotic history, patriotic music.

I looked around for a copy of the *Frankfurter Allgemeine Zeitung*. Ah – there it was, and there he was. I made a show of asking politely if the seat opposite was taken. Fabian made a show of reluctantly conceding that it was free.

He was in disguise.

The pinstriped suit was typical Departmental garb. But the wig? Last time I saw him Fabian had mousy brown hair. Today he was blond. With a military moustache that I knew was fake. Heavy horn-rimmed glasses. And an orange tan. He looked like a 35-year-old forex trader on a bad day.

Where did they get them from – RADA? I happened to know that Fabian was a PPE graduate from Corpus Christi, but he seemed to have missed his vocation. They all had. Can spying be called a vocation? I always thought of it as a trade for people who seemed normal, but weren't really.

Fabian eyed me. He didn't like me and we had nothing in common. He once told me that the Department had to use 'whatever it could get' in a place like Prague. This used to be

A Meeting with Fabian

true, which is why the Department contacted me in the first place. I wasn't offended. Well, maybe a bit.

But things had changed. Czechoslovakia's capital had been on the front line until 1989, when the thaw in East-West relations reduced it to a backwater. Today it was a key station once again. The city was crawling with Russians, who thought they could blend in. It was now very important for London to have ears and eyes in this tourist mecca.

We'd been a hot-spot, then a backwater, then a hot-spot again in less than thirty years. Can you have a hot-spot in a Cold War? I would have to ask a friend.

I ordered a coffee and put on my receptive face.

'What we need ...' drawled Fabian. I leant forward slightly, eyebrows raised, keenly alert, all ears.

'What we need at this point in time is – how can I put it ?– an established company, with a good trading record, a decent office and everything above-board with the Czech authorities, to act as – what shall I say? – the local base for ... certain operations ... which, of course, I cannot describe in *detail* but which ... will be made clearer in due course ... hmm?'

Fabian had a number of habits which made me want to hit him. A number? A lot. Ending his statements with 'hmm?' was top of the list. It meant: 'Are you intelligent enough to grasp what I am saying?' There was no way to react to his condescension, so I didn't.

'So ... let me ask ... for the record, you understand ... is Lanark Lighting absolutely *hunky dory* as far as permits, licences, authorizations, tax – all that sort of thing – is concerned? Hmm?'

'Yes'.

A Meeting with Fabian

'Very good, very good. As we thought, of course. But I'm sure you see why the question has to be asked in such ... shall we say ... sensitive circumstances? Hmm?'

'Yes'.

'Good, good. Let's move on, then. I am authorized to give you an initial outline of the Department's requirement'.

Fabian couldn't do an outline if his life was at stake. Wordy, circumlocutory, fond of euphemisms and lame metaphors. The real brief came from somewhere else in the Department, and what I was about to receive was the extended version.

I took out my cigarettes and then put them back in my pocket. The Czech Republic was the last country to ban smoking in public places. A bastion of liberty. But € 3.8 billion a year from the EU speaks with a loud voice, so the Czechs eventually gave in.

'The general picture is – as I'm sure you know – both complex and relatively fast-moving ...'

I fixed my eyebrows in position, leant a bit further forward and forced myself to maintain an expression of extreme interest and attention.

Time passed. Fabian's words flowed over and around me. I followed the advice of agony aunts to women engaged in carnal relations with an unloved lover. I thought of dinner ... should I try Pad Thai again? Could I get it right this time? I thought of Beaujolais, my black Labrador. How could I stop him chasing other dogs in the park? Would those lights arrive from Harlow in time? Would Galena be in a better mood tonight?

'... so I am sure you can understand – and I am speaking here not only for myself, but also on behalf of others in the Department, of course – that these are matters of the most extreme delicacy insasmuch as they may – *may*, I stress –

portend the possibility of a measure of – how to put it? – *embarrassment* to HMG if not handled with the requisite – let us say – *aplomb*. Hmm?'

Inasmuch? Portend? Aplomb? I had never heard a human being utter these words. Perhaps that's what you get from three years of PPE. What *was* PPE anyway? I had no idea. It seemed to be the ante-room to a career as a parliamentary advisor, but what exactly did they study? I speculated … the history of moral philosophy? How political systems function? But these seemed to be diametrically opposed. Economics? I remembered the old joke: 'Eleven of the last ten economic forecasts turned out to be wrong.' Was it a joke?

Fabian was still orating quietly. He wasn't looking at me, so he couldn't tell that I was lost in my own thoughts. He probably didn't care.

But I did. I had work to do.

'Fabian … I'm sorry to be blunt, but can we cut to the chase? I've got a business to run and – much as I value the privilege of lending a hand to HMG from time to time – I need to get back to the office. *What exactly is it that you want me to do?*'

Half an hour later Fabian wound a silk scarf round his throat (twice) and stood up. His handshake was – well, you know what it was like. But I had the Department's brief.

They wanted a base in Prague to shelter 'operatives' carrying out assassinations of political and industrial figures who were considered unhelpful by the powers-that-be, which meant the CIA. Lanark Lighting would provide that base, giving the Department deniability, and the Department would give the Americans all the deniability they could possibly want. Our roles were clear.

I went outside and lit up a Camel. Then another. I had a lot to think about. First and foremost, what was in it for me? I

A Meeting with Fabian

had a good business, a nice apartment, a girlfriend with a successful art gallery, a faithful dog ... what more did I need?

Something, obviously, or I would never have got tangled up in the Czech affairs of the Department in the first place. But what, exactly? Until now, it had just been a matter of setting up bank accounts and channelling funds. Book-work, admin, shell companies ... tricky, but neither arduous nor dangerous. No-one would ever mistake Ian McKerrell, with his khaki chinos and his green polo-neck, for one of the Department's operational staff.

I knew this because they made me wait for anything up to an hour on my rare visits to their gaudy headquarters on the South Bank. I was helping my country simply because I could and should. They paid a pittance, but that didn't matter. There could be no public recognition, but that didn't matter either. For the first time, I began to wonder what *did* matter? Why was I doing this? So far it had all been an interesting diversion, a bit like a hobby. But this was different.

Fabian was raising the stakes. This was the real thing. Could I? Should I?

I needed a chat with a higher power.

The Church of The Holy Nativity

I took a tram to the Church of The Holy Nativity in Mala Strana.

It was one of the Skoda 14T variants, popularly known as 'Porsche Trams'. Although brand-new, accelerating like a Tesla, it already had the distinctive smell of its thirty-year-old brethren … wet clothes, wet dog, soggy newspapers and the occasional whiff of Old Spice. There were plenty of seats but I showed that I was a native by choosing to stand.

I was on my way to see Father Dominic. He's not a typical cleric. Historian, author, philosopher, psychotherapist … he had lived in more countries and just *knew more* than anyone I had ever met. He liked to deliver lectures but could also give a simple answer if he thought that's what members of his flock needed.

But in other ways he *is* a typical Catholic priest. We never mention it. I sort-of understand him and he understands me.

He lived in an attic high up and at one side of the church. To reach it you had to walk through the nave and then duck under a lintel five feet high. There were a lot of worn stone steps.

The church was empty. This country had once been highly devout, but the communists put a stop to that. These days Czechs worshipped health and fitness.

I was transfixed as always by the sheer exuberance of the decoration … Gothic, Baroque, Renaissance, Rococo … six hundred years of religious art from the floor to the ceiling a hundred feet above my head. There was gold and silver everywhere, shining and sparkling among stone figures of saints, enormous paintings and huge tapestries whose bright colours were only just beginning to fade. It was a breathtaking display,

The Church of The Holy Nativity

and I thought – not for the first time – that those medieval prelates knew what they were doing. Just to stand there was to feel awe.

I reached Father Dominic's eerie, slightly out of breath. A big smile. He seemed to be expecting me. He was a large man. Not ascetic. I thought of him as Friar Tuck. I once tried to find out where he came from, but he was a master of obfuscation. Greece? Albania? Armenia? I didn't know and never would. There were rumours that he'd been some kind of partisan before joining the Benedictines. He may have started them himself.

'What now, Ian? Women again? It's usually something to do with the so-called fairer sex when you find time in your busy schedule to seek counsel from Holy Mother Church'.

Father Dominic was fond of reminding me that my attendance at his services was intermittent.

I mumbled something about patriotism, morals, a dilemma. I had no idea what I was really asking him. But he did.

'Ahah! I knew it! You've reached the grand old age of 45 and you've achieved everything that a normal human being could ever wish for in *material terms*. But there's something missing, isn't there?'

I had to nod.

'I've told you a hundred times that the spiritual outweighs the material by a factor of ten. If so-called 'happiness' is what you wish for. So now, with all the possessions you could conceivably desire, you feel a gap … a void … an absence of real meaning in your existence?'

Nod.

'We both know that the *real* answer – the *only* real answer – is to be found in the teachings of the Church. You have deviated from the true pathway – we both know this, but one lives

The Church of The Holy Nativity

in hope. Now you think that loyalty to your masters in London – the 'Department', I think you call it – could be the solution to your fervent wish for meaning in life?'

Nod.

'Then it's simple. You must give the Department your absolute and unswerving devotion, just as you would if you were following the true path to salvation via the Twelve Stations of the Cross. It will be good practice'.

Father Dominic opened a bottle of Glenfarclas Cask-Strength and we moved on to other topics. *I had been told*, which is why I was there. He had different ends in view.

'I think your young executive – what's his name? Andrew? has great promise. Very, very bright. I was wondering if a course of one-to-one seminars on the philosophical precepts of Martin Heidegger might possibly help him on his way to greater things?'

I frowned. Father Dominic shrugged. He was a realist. I finished my dram and left, thanking him for his advice and promising to attend confession soon.

He was right. All or nothing. There would be risks, but my life was devoid of risk or danger. Had I settled into the comfortable middle years without knowing it? I thought back to the mad days of my youth. How had any of us survived? Whatever I was then seemed to function without knowledge or intelligence, but I could still remember the excitement of simply being alive, blood racing, doing reckless things.

Perhaps someone had been watching over me? Would they still? I bowed to the altar on the way out.

I decided to go for it.

A Day at Work

I wake to the sound of *The Dam Busters March* on my phone. It's 6 am and Galena doesn't stir. (Galena – *nee* Helena – born Czech but hoping to seem more exotic). She won't greet the new day until 10 or 11 o'clock.

Coffee. Slice of toast. Feed Beaujolais, check his water-bowl. Empty. Take him out for a quick lamp-post check. At this time of morning the air is chilly and I huddle into my coat. Beaujolais couldn't care less. We walk up to the square and back again. The cobbled streets are wet and there's a cold wind. I've soon had enough. He wants more. I feel guilty. Give him a pat, blow Galena a kiss and set off for the office.

I like to be first in, but Svetlana usually beats me to it. I'm happy to concede defeat because it means more coffee, better than mine. I don't know how she does it but I'm glad she does.

8 am approaches and people start arriving, unwrapping scarves, hanging up coats and taking off sweaters. Prague winters can be brutal. There's no snow this year so there's no fun – just icy winds and slippery pavements. It could be Edinburgh.

I watch my Czechs getting ready for work and am struck, yet again, by their diligence. They seem to have a gene called 'nose to the grindstone'. In a technical business like mine you couldn't ask for more.

Svetlana comes in for diaries. We sit on the sofas opposite each other. Her expression is pert but she's wearing a very short skirt. I pretend not to notice. This is Svetlana's way. Her colleagues think of her as a *femme fatale* but it doesn't ring true to me and never has. She knows this.

It doesn't matter.

A Day at Work

We go through the calendar for the week ahead. These lights *here*, this rig *there*, these technicians *here,* these generators *there*, *this* director is being a pain, *that* director doesn't know what he's doing, *this* company could be a credit-risk, *that* company wants us to front four-star accommodation for its crews, *that* gaffer has been spotted lying in the gutter at 3am … and so on.

'Then there's something else that might interest you.' She looked past me at the window, an odd expression on her face.

'Really?' Tell me more!'

'Well … it's just someone I met at the Four Seasons. '

She flicked her hair.

'I don't know … it might be nothing … but he *said* he was planning to shoot the exteriors for the new *Mental* sequel here in Prague … and I said that I knew the best location lighting company in the whole country … and he gave me his card. It might be nothing …'

'Svetlana! Brilliant! This is a gilt-edged, numero uno, top-class new business lead! You're a genius! How did you leave it with him?'

She looked past me at the window.

'I'm not sure … we exchanged numbers and well … you know.'

'Svetlana! I spend my whole life trying to make contact with potential new clients and here *you* are … having a casual drink with someone at the Four Seasons … and bingo! You should have my job!'

She looked me square in the eyes at last.

'Well … yes, Ian. Maybe I could be of more help. In some capacity.'

Svetlana concentrated on her notes while I tried to come to terms with this idea.

11

A Day at Work

It took me a moment to gather my thoughts.

'Who is he?'

She fished in her handbag.

'His name is Harry Burger.'

Oh, no!

I knew all about Harry the Big Mac. Everyone did, Successful, but tainted. A legend, but as in Minotaur, not Hercules. I could guess what had happened. Should I ask? No. But I knew what *would* happen.

'Lana ... I don't often give you instructions, do I?'

She wasn't sure what I meant.

'No, Ian. Hardly ever.'

'OK. Good. Well ... *here is an instruction.* You will *not* meet Burger again, on any pretext or for any purpose whatsoever. Is that clear?'

'But why ... what do you mean?'

'Let me just say that I am thinking of your own good. You will *not* see him, communicate with him, answer emails or texts ... you will simply have *nothing to do with him*. Ever. Is that understood?'

'Yes, Ian.' She looked crestfallen.

I opened my drawer and put five 2,000 CZK notes in an envelope.

'And here is a small reward for your initiative.'

She looked at me, uncomprehending. Did I really have to tell her about Burger's track-record? Better not. The money and the instructions ought to be enough.

There was a moment while she composed herself and returned to the items on her schedule.

'OK, Ian. Then we have the question of these rigs on *Naplavka*. I don't think LeoMovies have got permission ...

A Day at Work

they say they have, but my contact at City Hall has never heard of them.'

I suggested that *my* contact at City Hall could iron it all out if I called her.

'Oh, can you? It would be so great!'

I leaned back, pleased with myself.

Solving all these problems was actually Andrew's job. He was very good at it. Svetlana was just making sure I was in the picture.

'And then there's Gideon …'

'What about him?'

'Well …' she looked away. 'We're supposed to be lighting his condom commercial in Studio 5, but I can't find any paperwork'. She looked back at me with a blank face.

'Oh, *that* …'

I'd told Gideon, an old friend, that we'd sort out the lights for his latest Cannes Award-Winner, but I'd forgotten to put the details into the system.

'*Mea culpa*!'

'What?'

'I mean it's my fault. Sorry. I'll brief Andrew.'

Svetlana gathered up her things and left the office. Her posture spoke volumes. It was *not* acceptable for the boss to do private deals with his mates *unless* they were entered into the system in the proper way.

I hurried after her.

'Svetlana! I'm really sorry! I'll explain it all to Andrew and then I – or he – will upload the details. I'm sorry, honestly! I just forgot.'

'I'm sure *Andrew and I* will be able to put things back in order.'

A Day at Work

I thought again about my Czechs. They revered 'the system' – any system - in a way that Brits couldn't and didn't want to. *We* took pleasure in learning the rules and subverting them. *They* took pride in learning the rules and abiding by them.

Svetlana interrupted my musing with a fresh cup of coffee. All smiles again.

'Ian. Can I just say … I *very much* appreciate this bonus. I don't think I deserve it. This man was on the hook! He was going to sign us up! But … you tell me to cut him off!'

'Lana … what can I say? Am I older than you?'

'Yes … well, maybe a little bit.'

'Is it possible that I know more about this business than you do?'

She pouted in a way that said yes, but with reservations.

'*Svetlana!* Trust me. This man is notorious. He's an animal. If he were to get physical with you I have no idea what would happen!'

She raised one eyebrow. I didn't know what she meant, but I would think back later to this conversation.

The day went on. Very much like other days. People came in to ask for an opinion or a decision. I spent most of my time in the phone, talking to clients or people I wanted to be clients.

Andrew popped his head round the door at 12.30. 'Fancy a pint?'

We strolled back at 3 pm, on top of the world. Our Czechs didn't look up from their screens as we sauntered into the office. They'd all taken a one-hour lunch-break, timed to the minute.

Back in my room, I wondered what it meant if a couple of pints with Andrew was the highlight of my working day. I had to admit that the routine was boring. I was a middle-aged,

A Day at Work

middle-class middle-man. It was a far cry from my dreams of fighter-pilot glory as a young boy in Lanark.

Back then, we were all the same. Ceilings covered in Airfix models, lovingly painted. Shelves full of World War Two comics: *'Eagle', 'Lion', 'Air Ace' 'Commando'* ... A weekly trip to the Regal to see *'Bridge On The River Kwai', 'The Guns Of Navarone', 'The Longest Day'*...

I must have been an easy target for the Department's recruiters. There was something missing, and they seemed to know it.

Or were we *all* still the same ... stuck with our mortgages and pension plans, kitchen improvements and holidays in the Aegean, but still clutching fantasies of fire and fury in the face of the enemy?

I was brought up on British heroics. Like most of my friends, I'd been indoctrinated since the day I was born.

Licence to Kill

I grew up with James Bond. Sean Connery, Roger Moore ... pretend psychopaths with a sense of humour and nice clothes. We all knew that Ian Fleming worked in secret intelligence during the war, so we never doubted that what he wrote as fiction was, in fact, fact.

True, 007 lived an improbably glamorous existence. Beautiful women fell like ninepins, gothic villains threatened to destroy civilization, Bond came within a hair's-breadth of horrible death at least once in every movie ... but this was just artistic licence, surely.

Reality intruded when a string of American traitors was exposed: Walker, Ames, Hanssen, Myers, Pitts ... a parade of losers. They were variously overweight, bald and down-at-heel. Then the sleazy story of the Cambridge Four (or Five) was revealed here at home: patrician drunks and oddballs with the morals of a whelk.

Which one was a faithful portrait of the world of spies and double-agents? Like many others of my age, I preferred to think that it was James Bond. Philby and Co were freaks, letting the side down in more ways than one.

So when a well-dressed stranger struck up a conversation at Soho House one evening, making oblique references to national security, my ears pricked up and I felt a tremor of excitement. He was a good conversationalist and I'm a good listener, so we went upstairs to dinner together.

He seemed to know a lot about me, which strengthened my conviction that he was, as I suspected, a representative of the secret services. He chatted away about the affairs of the day, Czech politics and Chelsea's chances. He even knew something about film lighting. When we said good-bye he gave me his card and invited me to call the next day.

I did (of course) and that afternoon found myself in the Vauxhall Lego building where SIS hides in plain sight. There were three of them: my new friend of last night and two others, equally well-turned-out in dark suits and looking for all the world like serious, middle-ranking civil servants. Which is, I suppose, what they were.

'We won't beat about the bush' said the one I took to be their leader.

'We know *a little bit* about you, Mr McKerrell' (they all smiled at this) 'and it seems to us, other things being equal, that you are particularly well-placed to render useful services to Her Majesty's Government – should you, of course, be so inclined…'

Three pairs of politely-raised eyebrows.

'Well … yes …. of course … I mean, I think that goes without saying, doesn't it?'

I had to admit that I was flattered. This was my first brush with the world of 007, something I never thought would happen in a million years. I wasn't just flattered, I was exhilarated.

'It's good to hear you say that' said the third member of their team. 'Not everyone does. Nowadays, quite a few people in your age-group feel the exact opposite.'

'Oh … yes, I suppose so' I said, thinking of old friends who'd expressed contempt, almost hatred for the United Kingdom and its institutions. Not just left-wingers, and not just Scotsmen, either. Strangely, there was no-one like this in the Prague ex-pat community. Maybe distance lent charm. Maybe absence makes the heart grow fonder. Maybe seeing how other countries function sheds a positive light on the UK,

Licence to Kill

for all its defects. I was aroused from this reverie by Senior Man.

'Good. Can I give you a rough outline of the kind of thing you might be able to do for HMG and this service in particular?'

'Yes please'.

They spoke for an hour. Fluent, logical, organized. I was one of hundreds, probably thousands, to have passed this way.

What it all amounted to was setting up shell companies, channelling funds, arranging payments, providing certain kinds of information, and from time to time providing 'cover' for personnel they needed to send to Prague without arousing undue attention.

I said that this all seemed to be within my capacities as someone well-established in the Prague film industry, with – as they obviously knew – a good trading record and a reputable, if low-profile, name in my small corner of the movie production business.

'You might be wondering *why now*?' said Number Two.

I wasn't. It seemed obvious. After decades of entente, détente, stand-offs, agreements – all the diplomatic paraphernalia of the Cold War – the Czech Republic was once again a front-line country, and Prague was a city where the Russians could keep their ears to the ground.

'Things are hotting up.' His colleagues gave him a pained expression.

'The Russians see Prague as an important listening-post. Like Vienna, but more so. It's all been a bit back-seat since Havel, but now 'the bear' seems to be waking up from hibernation.'

He seemed pleased with this figure of speech. Everyone smiled again.

'Can't imagine why' said my friend – Number Three – sardonically.

'Quite … but, whatever the reasons, our allies feel that our levels of alertness and – particularly – 'humint' – need to be raised quickly and by a considerable degree. And we – by which I mean Europe, Britain and the Department – are the people on the spot.'

As I had thought. Our instructions were coming from the other side of the Atlantic, as they had done since 1942. This was what the 'special relationship' meant. *They* had power and money, *we* had very little of either.

From this point on, the Department (as they liked to call it) became a central, if not major, part of my working life. There would be long periods of silence, then a flurry of demands. Then more silence. I got my instructions in code, if they were simple, or from Fabian if they were complicated. I prayed for simple instructions.

I never knew the 'bigger picture'. I didn't need to know, so I wasn't told. One of the legacies of Philby and his friends was that everyone worked in a haze of ignorance, doing their bit but deprived of knowledge that wasn't deemed essential to their function. I didn't mind. I was a small cog in the Department's machine, but a happy cog.

The work needed an eye for detail, but – though I say it myself – this is my strong point. It was not unlike what we did at Lanark Lighting: make sure that *this* combination of lights and peripheral kit arrives at *this* location on *this* date, at *this* time, with *these* technicians in attendance, then make sure that everything and everyone goes away when the job is finished. Then make sure that every item and every hour is invoiced and paid within 30 days. Detail.

Licence to Kill

I couldn't speak to anyone about it, not even Galena. *Certainly* not Galena. My only 'human interface' was Fabian, which was like talking to a turbot. It didn't matter. It might be grunt-work but it was *secret*, and that gave me a private thrill. I wasn't James Bond – *don't be ridiculous!* – but I might be, in a small way, Q.

This looked different.

Andrew Lloyd

It was all too easy to understand why Father Dominic wanted to coach my 'young executive'. Andrew Lloyd was one of those unusual people who seem to have it all. He was good-looking, cheerful, charming and likeable. He was a natural athlete, as fit as a flea. He was also extremely bright.

It was the first attribute which explained Father Dominic's interest but the last that made me wonder why he'd joined the Royal Marines. A high IQ usually meant Artillery, Signals or even tanks (though hardly ever Intelligence). But he'd chosen the Marines, and got perfect scores on his Commando Course. He seemed all set for a fast-track military career, but then he'd left and gone into the theatre.

I'd asked him why at his interview.

'Hard to say. I loved the Marines. All my family were bootnecks so joining was a no-brainer. But after a while I suppose I felt there must be more to life … I'd always been a fan of the theatre, ever since I was taken to 'Puss In Boots' at the age of five… the roar of the greasepaint, the smell of the crowd, as they say … sorry, too much information.'

'No, not at all. I'm just curious how you ended up wanting to work for a film lighting company in Prague. Though 'ended up' isn't quite right, is it? You're only half my age.'

'I thought I'd be an actor. I went round the country, as you do, playing bit-parts in rep while I learnt the basics. But I was never Puss. The best I got was one of Colin's sisters. I went to countless auditions. In the end I realised I just didn't have what it takes to be a leading man. Whatever that is. Meanwhile, I'd been getting more and more interested in stage management, specially the technical side of things. So here I am.'

'And Prague?'

'Oh, I came here with a couple of friends and was … what's the right word? … captivated. I'd never seen anywhere like it. I thought: well, if you've got to live somewhere, why not here? It's as simple as that.'

Good answer. I'd have said the same thing myself.

I liked this young man. 'Fancy a pint?'

Down the stairs, out and round the corner. The Blue Lion. They had Cerna Hora.

We raised our glasses, nodded to each other and took a drink.

'Well now', I said. 'Let's begin with religion and politics.'

Andrew looked startled. Was I joking?

'That'll be a short conversation' he said. 'I've got no interest in either.'

'What – none at all?'

'Near as makes no difference. I was forced to go to Sunday School – weren't we all? – but the only bit I liked was the Nativity Play.'

'Joseph?'

'No. Can't you guess? A shepherd if I was lucky'.

'Not a Wise Man?'

'No. *They* had to move around the stage to present their gifts. I was condemned to stand still at the back looking rustic.'

'Maybe that's what inspired your thespian ambitions.'

'Could be. I hadn't thought… but that was years later. All I cared about at school was joining the Marines.'

'Peace on Earth to all men.'

'Is that a quotation?'

'Probably. But I'm not so hot on the Bible myself, I must admit, though I was brought up as a Roman Catholic.'

'Were you, now? I've always thought you guys had the right idea – drama, ceremony, ritual, fantastic décor, Latin, costumes, imagery …'

'You make it sound like a theatrical production!'

'Well, yes … but isn't it? If you want to give people a sense of the infinite, or whatever it's called, that's not a bad way to go about it.'

I thought about the Church of the Holy Nativity and Father Dominic. Could I do that to Andrew? No, I couldn't.

'Politics, then. No leanings, affiliations, memberships? Isn't everyone supposed to be a socialist until they're twenty-five?'

'I've heard that, but remember - I didn't go to university. When my mates from school were waving placards I was learning how to cross a river with a 31-pound pack.'

'Where did you grow up?'

'That's another factor, I suppose. Dartmoor. People didn't talk about politics. They just voted conservative as their parents and grandparents did. Of course, I came across a variety of political views in the theatre … or was it a variety? … but by then I was much more interested in stagecraft – which is obviously a million miles away from politics.'

He grinned.

Andrew was a great success in the office. He was a great success with our clients. He was a great success with the surly technicians at the studios. Beaujolais, the Labrador, liked him. Everyone liked him.

Galena, my girlfriend, took a shine to Andrew at once. This was strange because she didn't usually approve of anyone unless they belonged to an oppressed minority. I'd always wondered how this applied to me, but I'd never had the nerve to ask.

Andrew Lloyd

Andrew became a regular guest at our apartment. Dinner, Sunday lunch, drinks parties with my clients and Galena's friends. He turned out to be an asset at Galena's art gallery, helping her design exhibitions.

'He has such an artistic eye!' she said, giving me an eye which was anything but artistic. But I knew my place: solid provider, feet on the ground, while Galena whirled and ricocheted in her universe of ideas, causes, images and creativity.

After Fabian's 'briefing' I knew I had to say something to Andrew. We would soon have two strange bods in the office and it would take Andrew five minutes to figure out they weren't what they were supposed to be. But how to bring him into the picture without compromising the Department?

I thought of a devious plan. My friend Alasdair ran a security company in Prague. I would tell Andrew we were providing a covert home for a couple of Alasdair's people for a few days, all off the record and off the books. Very hush-hush.

That would work. Or so I hoped.

My New Colleagues

'The Gaffer from Hanwell and his Best Boy are here to see you' trilled Svetlana. She cocked a hip and leered. This wasn't for my benefit. I wasn't her type, and we both knew it.

'Please send them in'.

Little and Large came through the door. One was over six foot and could have played lock for Swansea (I found out later he once did). The other was small and unimpressive. They both wore M & S suits and colourful ties. I thought: 'Oh dear. Blending in 101 ... how did they miss that module on their training course at Hambleside?'

Large was all smiles and affability. 'So nice of you to spare the time ... been very much looking forward to meeting you ... awfully glad we could hook up at last – we know how busy you must be ...'

Little said nothing at all.

'Oh, yes ... my Best Boy here doesn't say a lot ... he's from Glasgow, you know ... silent but deadly. Solid chap. Worth his weight in gold ... utterly reliable ... tower of strength ...'

Large burbled on. Svetlana brought coffee. Large followed her with his eyes as she sashayed out. The Best Boy looked at nothing.

My visitors were Fabian's hit-men. It would be my job to provide them with cover. My heart sank. Hit-men? Really?

Then I thought: well, what would a government assassin look like? I had no idea. Would he be a Mafia-style thug, all bulky and aggressive? Probably not. Or would he be a Smiley-type figure, no different from the ordinary man in the street? If so, that's what I had sitting in front of me.

We began the formalities. Lanark Lighting was supposedly employing these two on a short-term contract for a commercial one of our clients was filming at Barrandov. They couldn't tell a spotlight from an LED, but as long as the paperwork was in order our cover was as secure as it needed to be.

Large turned out to be called Hackworth. At least, his passport said so. I knew the Department had given him the identity of someone whose life had ended prematurely somewhere like Barnsley. His real name was no concern of mine. The 'Best Boy', though, was probably really called McCoig. No-one cared, and he seemed to know it.

Familiar territory. I myself had three passports. The Department were very good at false IDs. But so was everyone else. A plausible fake would survive two days at most if anyone was taking an interest.

Large (Hackworth) made an effort. 'Very nice place you've got here. It must be centuries old. You can almost feel the history in the air … I bet these rooms have seen a thing or two in their time …'

I looked around and tried to see the place through his eyes. He was correct. Not a right-angle in sight. High ceilings with their original plaster mouldings and traces of 18th-century coloured motifs. Solid doors with heavy, iron handles. Wide, oak floorboards with complicated mosaic designs in the corners. Casements revealing the thickness of the walls, which in this room was nearly two metres.

We were lucky. Lanark Lighting occupied some of the most enviable offices in the city. All thanks to my friendship with a property developer who suffered from depression. When things got too much he would appear in my office for a glass of Glenmorangie and a bit of amateur psychotherapy. Whenever it was time for a rent review I took him up to Barrandov to rub shoulders with the stars. It usually worked.

My New Colleagues

I wanted Hackworth to feel at home. 'Yes, this area is history wall-to-wall. And I do mean wall ... that one, for instance, goes back to the 14th century.'

'No way!'

'Yes way. If we have time for a walk while you're here I can show you where Mozart gave the premiere of his Prague Symphony.'

'No! Mozart? I thought he lived in Ebury Street, just next to that 24-hour garage?'

'He did. He lived all over Europe during his short life. He stayed in this city several times. He loved Prague and Prague loved him. But I can also show you a brothel ...'

'Oh yes ... we know all about that. Stag parties and so on.'

'That's not what I mean at all.'

I was feeling prim, as I always did when Prague was seen as a synonym for cheap sex. After all, I came from Lanark.

'I'm talking about a slice of *real history*. It's in a narrow street just behind this building. 'The Red Peacock' was patronized by Bismarck, Mahler and Kafka.'

'Kafka?' Hackworth was agog. 'Bismarck? No! You just don't think of them doing ... that kind of thing.'

'Well, they did. Quite often. Anyway, I can show you the very place. It's still there, with the same name, but these days it's a café.'

'That'll be something to tell the chaps back at the Department.'

I felt I ought to extend the hand of friendship to my new colleagues.

'Anyone fancy a beer?'

The Golden Lion

We trotted down the spiral staircase, crossed the road and found a table at The Golden Lion. Kozel on draft. A cheerful waiter took our order and was back in seconds with three half-litres of my favourite brew.

I thought they'd like The Golden Lion, because I did. From the outside it was three hundred years old but the inside, like everywhere in Prague, was comfortable and efficient. The PA system played hits from the 80s and 90s.

Prague's older citizens were divided in their musical preferences. It was either Depeche Mode or Black Sabbath.

'Well', I began as we raised our glasses. 'We ought to start by getting on first-name terms'.

I looked at McCoig. He said nothing.

'Oh, don't mind McCoig' said Hackworth jovially. 'No-one knows his first name. We all just call him McCoig'.

'OK. And yourself?'

Hackworth blushed. Avoiding my eyes, he mumbled: 'Adrian'.

I nearly snorted into my beer.

'We need to discuss your cover while you're at Lanark Lighting.'

Hackworth agreed. 'The Department said something about a TV commercial'.

'I think it'll work. Technically, you're the man in charge and McCoig is your assistant. But we obviously don't want you going anywhere near the set …'

Hackworth looked disappointed.

'I'd been looking forward to it!'

Could he mean it? Then I remembered that the 'magic of the movies' affected everyone from Nobel Prize-winners to supermarket shelf-stackers. Everyone except me.

'OK … if you just want to have a look … I can take you round …'

He brightened.

'But you two need to be based here, doing something that won't arouse any curiosity. *I know* – you can be planners. That means you won't have to produce anything at all – just sit at your laptops and look busy.'

'Yes!' said Hackworth, waggling his fingers to indicate keyboard skills. 'And if we're doing *planning* no-one will want to talk to us, either. We know all about *planners* – the Department's full of them.'

'I'll brief you on the rudiments, just in case anyone strikes up a conversation on the stairs. But it's best if you act as if it's all very hush-hush.'

'But it is.'

'No, what I mean is … oh, never mind'.

I hoped they understood. Of course they did. They were professionals.

'Apart from that, the less *I* know the better. I don't want to know who, how or when. You'll be here for a few days, I'll create paperwork proving you're involved with a commercial production, and the next thing *I'll* know will be an invoice from Pinewood Tech Support – or something like that – which I'll pay at the end of the month. But don't worry …'

Neither of them looked worried.

'It will be reimbursed, together with my modest honorarium, in St Helier.'

The Golden Lion

They couldn't care less, and why should they. In unison, they drained their glasses. Fresh half-litres arrived at once, Czech-style.

There was a pause.

'It's Stepan Sokol' blurted Hackworth.

'WHAT?'

'Sokol. You know – the arms dealer.'

I certainly did know. Sokol was one of the richest men in the country. He was infamous for amassing millions in obscure ways, but also famous for pouring some of those millions into Czech sports teams. He was the nearest thing to a national hero you could get in the Czech Republic.

'*Sokol?*' I whispered. 'Are you serious?

'Those are the orders' said Hackworth.

'You must realise he's got personal security that makes the Wagner Group look like schoolchildren?'

'We know', said Hackworth happily. 'We know all about that. But Orange Section have found an Achilles' Heel.'

Orange Section was the Department's research unit.

Hackworth could not stop talking. He was a chatterbox. How on earth had he been picked for an assignment like this? Or any? Even *I* knew that silence, evasion and pseudonyms were the Department's golden rules.

'Wild swimming' beamed Hackworth.

I must have looked puzzled.

'Wild swimming. That's the Achilles' Heel. Every morning. In his private lake near Tabor. No bodyguards. Just him and a towel.'

'Don't tell me. I don't want to know. I *mustn't* know.'

'Well … you *have* to know because we need your help.'

'You've got my help. I'm providing you with an office and a cover-story to explain why two middle-aged Brits have flown into Prague, done nothing and flown out again.'

'There's something else.'

'What is it?'

'Well …' Hackworth blushed again. 'We need you to drive us down there.'

'What? Why me? Why can't you just rent a car and drive yourselves?'

Hackworth went even pinker.

'Because we can't drive.'

It took me a few moments to think this through. 'Why not?'

'I had a licence but I'm afraid I lost it for …' mumble mumble … 'and it will be six months before I get it back again.'

'What about him?' McCoig was staring vacantly at the ceiling.

'Never had one. Never took the test.'

I looked from one to the other. Hackworth seemed faintly embarrassed. McCoig betrayed no emotion of any kind.

I began to wonder. They couldn't *drive*? What else couldn't they do? What *could* they do?

'OK. Let's meet up at 9.30 tomorrow at the office'.

I needed to think. I was what the Department called a 'facility' – an expat who could, for patriotic reasons, provide various humdrum services which HMG might occasionally find useful. I was definitely *not* operational. This was a whole new ball-game … a completely different kettle of fish … and probably a bag of worms.

The mist was coming up from the river as I walked home. My footsteps sounded very loud in the narrow, medieval streets. There was hardly anyone about, and I buttoned up my coat against the chill.

Prague was always surprising. One moment you were in a busy street full of iPhone shops and fashion stores ... turn a corner and you were tripping over cobbles that had been there since men wore swords.

Should I have taken Hackworth and McCoig out for something to eat? No. A couple of beers, but that was it. I wanted to stay as far away from these clowns as possible.

Was it possible? From the sound of things, maybe not. Well, we would see. Meanwhile, they might not be able to drive but they could certainly find their own dinner.

Barrandov

I'd promised Hackworth a trip to the studios.

Galena wasn't pleased. 'Here I am slaving away to get the exhibition ready and here *you* are skiving off to lech at movie-stars!'

Skive? Lech? Who had she been talking to?

But a promise is a promise.

We jumped in my old Volvo and headed south. It was only twenty minutes. Round the hairpins, up the motorway past the fossil cliff, through a hillside estate of 19th-century villas and there it was: Europe's largest movie studio complex, founded by Vaclav Havel's dad. This is where the Czech film production industry had exploded onto the world scene in the sixties and where hundreds of foreign movies had been made since 1990, all taking advantage of Czech talent and Czech prices.

Lanark Lighting was a small part of this enterprise.

Hackworth's eyes were shining.

'Come on, then. Let's have a prowl around.'

I had no idea what was filming but no matter. My face was so well-known by now that I didn't need to show my pass. We went into Stage One, just because it was nearest, and stood at the back.

Hackworth struck lucky. It was DiCaprio and Jennifer Lawrence. They were wearing armour. It was probably yet another epic set in 300 BC or 3,000 AD. As usual, there was a lot of standing around while technicians adjusted things, then 'action' for half a minute. Then a lot more standing around. I observed the lighting crew. Not impressed. Not mine.

But Hackworth didn't care. He was in Seventh Heaven. 'Did you see how DiCaprio missed his marks on that first

Barrandov

take?' he chortled. 'Gosh – wait till I tell the guys in the Department about *this*!'

It was quite touching, in a way. Like a ten-year-old on a school visit. I had to remind myself that Hackworth was here to kill someone.

We were standing in the shadows at the back of the soundstage. No-one could see us. I became aware of a figure on the edge of my vision, someone wearing a business suit who belonged here even less than we did. I glanced in his direction.

'Don't worry', said Hackworth. 'Clocked.'

After a while the figure came closer, till he was standing right behind us.

'I have a message for you' he said in a gruff voice. I thought I'd be witty and tell him that casting for Godfather 4 was in the next building. But Hackworth beat me to it.

'Oh, hi!' he said in his usual friendly manner. 'I was wondering when you'd turn up!'

The stranger looked surprised. 'You don't know who I am.'

'True, true … but I know what you are and why you're here. We are very pleased to see you. It's great to have the chance of a private chat, isn't it?'

The stranger seemed baffled, as I was.

'But we can't talk here' said Hackworth in a stage whisper. 'Let's pop outside for a quick *perekurushka*. How does that sound?' All smiles.

'We'll leave Gunter to mind the shop. He's got to make sure that DiCaprio doesn't get too fresh with Lawrence.' Hackworth laughed, as usual, at his own joke.

Ten minutes later Hackworth was back. 'Can we see anything else while we're here?'

'Yes, of course. We've got all morning.'

Barrandov

We left Stage One and made our way up the road to Building Three, a giant hangar containing Studios 5,6 and 7.

We looked inside. There was Gideon, my client, with a film crew and a condom the size of a Zeppelin floating in mid-air. Underneath it a crowd of half-naked young women gyrated while a chap in his underpants seemed to be abseiling down to their waiting arms. I took Hackworth's elbow and hustled him outside.

'What's wrong?' he asked.

'*That*, Adrian, was your cover! We nearly blew it!'

We strolled further along the road.

'Post-production is a big thing at Barrandov,' I said. As it happens, it's something of an interest of mine. Would you like to see how it's done? The Foley unit is just up here.'

Hackworth looked sheepish.

'Not really' he admitted. 'I know what it means, of course, but ... what I *really* like are the stars ... the big names, the red carpets, the autographs, the Oscars ... the technical side doesn't ring my bell, to be honest.'

We did no better at Stage 4. They were making something in Czech. Hackworth's shoulders drooped.

'I expect you speak this lingo by now' he said.

It was my turn to look sheepish.

'I should, shouldn't I? But I don't. I tried. We all did when we got here. It's just too difficult, at least for me. Most of us speak 'Combat Czech' – we can be polite, order a beer and give taxi-drivers directions. But that's about it.'

'Never mind' he said. 'That's exactly what it's like for me anywhere north of Birmingham.' He laughed uproariously. I smiled politely.

I resolved to sign up again for Czech lessons the very next week.

Barrandov

By now we'd visited the big stages and began re-tracing our steps.

On the way I asked Hackworth what had happened to our man with a message.

He didn't reply – just nodded towards a yellow dumpster by the side of the road.

I didn't ask any more questions. I began to think that Hackworth must be a lot more, or perhaps a lot less, than he appeared to be.

But Hackworth was Hackworth, and couldn't stop talking.

'Where did they do the post-production for Casino Royale?' Can I see? Where did Goebbels meet Lida Baarova? Can you show me? On and on.

I did my duty as a tour-guide, not for the first time, with simulated interest. I had long ago lost my admiration for movies and film-actors. Maybe it was like a sausage: once you see how they're made, you never eat another.

Sir Michael Caine was the single exception.

But Hackworth was having the time of his life. Question after question after question. If I didn't know the answer I made it up. He neither knew nor cared. It was like escorting a schoolboy round the Car Show, and I felt oddly pleased that he was having fun.

He was as strange as a human being could be, but one way or another I would be relying on him when we set off for Tabor. I began to feel very nervous when he sent me an Instagram link the next morning: @ManOfMystery. I had to look. 'Undercover Agent Peeks Behind the Silver Screen'. Was this insane carelessness or brilliant camouflage? I crossed my fingers.

Cassandra

I'd been working late. Galena was preparing her exhibition at the gallery. Beaujolais would be pining for his dinner. Would he have got regular meals while roaming the savannah in a pack of proto-Labradors? Of course not. But maybe dogs had changed their expectations after 30,000 years of living with humans.

The street was full of people hurrying somewhere else, heads down, woolly hats pulled low. I could hear my mam say: 'Don't forget your bunnet, young man!' I put mine on.

What lay ahead of me tonight? I'd got a nice Vindaloo in the freezer. Beaujolais would need a good half-hour round the square, or perhaps down by the river, where there were squirrels. Then Galena would stomp in, grumpy, with a litany of complaints about her colleagues, her technicians, her customers, the Prague art market, the world…

As I walked through Wenceslas Square I glimpsed a familiar figure ahead of me. It was McCoig, all alone and walking quickly. What was he doing, and where was Hackworth? I decided to follow him. I couldn't say why. I just felt instinctively that he was bad news.

He marched up Vaclavske namesti and turned right into Ve Smeckach. Now I knew where he was going. 'Le Chiffre', one of Prague's many 'gentlemen's clubs'.

For some people Prague is synonymous with stag parties, cheap beer and cut-price sex. People who live here hardly notice – just as Londoners walking through Soho are blind to the shopfronts offering peep-shows, French models and intimate curiosities.

I never noticed Prague's sex industry after living here so long. I didn't want to. But I knew where it was.

Cassandra

McCoig went up the steps into the club. I waited fifteen minutes, then followed. Sign in, pay 2,000 CZK, get a bracelet and a locker key. Cheerful receptionists, with a couple of heavies in the background. All very civilized.

I walked up the stairs into the changing-room. It was spotless, with a white-coated female attendant swabbing the floor. It made me smile – whatever else they might be doing, Czechs revere the goddess of hygiene.

I had a shower and put on the bathrobe and slippers from my locker. I didn't know what to do next, but the attendant saw I was at a loss and pointed out the entrance. More stairs, then… an enormous space, stretching over two floors, dimly-lit, with bars and seating-areas on several levels, chrome and satin, all decorated like an oligarch's yacht. I was impressed, even though I tried not to be.

The air was fragrant with … something. I was no good at fragrances. But I knew what I could hear … the soft sound of Smetana's *Piano Trio*. The meaning was clear. This is a classy place. Behave! As if to reinforce the message, a couple of large men with short hair were wandering aimlessly around, seemingly with nothing much to do.

I looked about me. The room had the atmosphere of a millionaires' club, as its name suggested. But it was full of middle-aged men in dressing-gowns and young women wearing almost nothing.

It was clearly a *place of assignation*. Bismarck and Kafka would have felt at home.

I didn't get it. I couldn't see the attraction. But what did I know? This was an *industry*. I felt, not for the first time, that something important in life had passed me by.

Everywhere I looked were sofas, couches and banquettes occupied by men with slightly glazed expressions and lissom

Cassandra

young women – the only word was 'nubile' – talking to them animatedly. Everyone seemed to be happy. The customers really were. The women were very good actors. Or so it seemed to me.

As I watched, couples left the main area and headed off to – who knew where? Wherever it was, somewhere in the recesses of the building, it must be where the 'action' took place and the real money changed hands. I thought of Hieronymus Bosch. Then I caught myself. This wasn't hell on earth. As far as I could tell, everyone in view was a willing participant and pleased to be there.

I didn't know what to think.

I didn't know what to do, either, so I wandered over to a bar and sat down. At once, a fully-dressed female bar-person smiled, put a coaster in front of me and asked what I wanted. 'Gin and tonic, please'. Better to play safe. Is G & T alcoholic? I have my doubts. Alasdair has none. He would give it to his children if he had any.

Within a minute two half-naked women had occupied the stools either side of me. Where to look? I said hello to both, trying to appear exactly what I was – a newcomer who didn't know the ropes. As if at a secret signal, one of them disappeared. A dark-haired creature with a fringe, intelligent eyes and high cheekbones remained. She wore a short skirt and nothing else. I tried to focus my gaze on her face. She noticed and smiled.

'My name's Cassandra. What's yours?'

'Agamemnon. But my friends call me Aggie'.

I was trying to be clever, but she got it.

'Huh. I probably shouldn't be sitting with you, then. Is your wife around?

I was intrigued. This was unexpected.

Cassandra

'I'm sorry ... how did you know what I was talking about? I hope I'm not being rude.'

'Well, you are and you aren't. We could talk about classical Greek legends all evening if you wanted to, but ... I don't think that's what you're here for. Is it?'

I could hardly tell her why I was there. It certainly wasn't what she imagined. But then she wasn't what I'd expected, either.

I needed to look like everyone else while I scanned the room for McCoig. What to do? Money might be the answer.

'Can I suggest a deal?'

Raised eyebrows, looking as sceptical as a twenty-year-old can.

'No, I mean it. Tell me – what do you normally earn for half an hour talking to a punter like me?'

A real smile this time.

'It depends what happens!'

'Name a figure.'

'Oh, I don't know ... probably 4,000, or something like that ... all according to what happens next, of course ...'

I gave her 5,000.

'Now – do you mind if we just talk for half an hour? What do you want to drink?'

The 'champagne' had already arrived. Cassandra sipped hers. I left mine but handed over my credit card. Then I asked: 'How *did* you know what I was talking about?'

'Because I'm doing archaeology at Charles University.'

I was dying to ask why she was working at Le Chiffre, but I didn't want to be intrusive. Or a cliché: 'What's a nice girl like you doing in a place like this?' I might get an answer or I might get a slap in the face. For all I knew, this was a normal

Cassandra

way to pay your tuition fees in the Czech Republic. Come to think of it, it might be normal in Glasgow.

'Tell me, then … did Troy actually exist? Or was the Iliad a mish-mash of poetic tales from five hundred years before Homer was born?'

'Phew!' She began talking. Just as I had hoped. This was perfect cover for me to look round discreetly and try to spot McCoig.

It didn't take long.

Cassandra was talking about the Bronze Age Collapse.

On the level below us was an S-shaped couch. On the couch was McCoig. On McCoig was a good-looking blonde, simulating rhapsody. On either side were two more young women, stroking his arms and apparently waiting their turn.

This told me all I wanted to know. The man was a flake. A liability. This was certainly *not* how Departmental employees were meant to behave on duty – especially when their mission was 'sensitive'.

I got up to go. Cassandra had reached Schliemann. 'Thief, publicity-seeker, wrecker – he cared *nothing* about historical truth, he thought *only* about making a name for himself … he ruined the site of Troy for generations of real archaeologists who came later …'

Her cheeks were pink and her voice had gone up a notch.

I thought how interesting it would be to have a real discussion with her.

I gave her my card.

'Cassandra … if you'd like to talk about this again, I'd love to meet you somewhere else … perhaps a restaurant, or maybe a bar …'

It seemed she'd heard this before. She turned away and looked cross.

Cassandra

'I mean it …'

No answer.

She wasn't here for conversation. She was here to earn money as quickly and painlessly as possible.

I was a waste of time.

I made my way towards the exit and heard a voice behind me:

'Bye, bye, *Aggie*.'

I walked home thinking how sad it was that someone like 'Cassandra' had to make ends meet at Le Chiffre. But did *she* see it that way? I had no idea.

What I *did* know was that McCoig was a menace, and I ought to tell someone.

But who? There was no point saying anything to Hackworth. He was McCoig's partner. Who, then? It had to be Fabian. My heart sank. Was there another way? No, there wasn't.

'Hello, Nautilus. This is Oyster.'

'Ha ha ha. You chaps *do* make me laugh. It's a clear line, but I must say I'm very glad to see, *very* glad to see, that you read the SOPs and abide by them … ha ha ha … even when it's not strictly necessary in order to safeguard Departmental communication security. Ha ha ha.'

Fabian was a fool.

I waited for the 'Hmm?' but there was silence.

'OK – do you want to know why I'm calling?'

'Ian, yes, of course. Yes. It's obviously something important, or perhaps we should say *pertinent*. I'm sure that even in a place like Prague you chaps have better things to do than phone up just to pass the time of day, ha ha ha. Hmm?'

He didn't mean to rile me. He just did. This was Fabian's idea of how 'chaps' spoke to each other. I wondered, yet again, how someone so maladroit could be responsible for keeping people like me motivated.

'It's McCoig'.

'I *think* I have some vague awareness, – fairly dim, admittedly – of the operative whereof you speak … I seem to remember Glasgow, or somewhere like that … are we, as they say these days, *on the same page?*'

'Yes. And I want you to get him out of Prague as soon as you can'.

'Ian … Ian … this isn't like you. It isn't like you at all. I think of you as cool, calm and collected … very suitable for somewhere like Prague ha ha ha … but here you are telling me – I might even say *commanding* me – to stand down an operative who is already fully engaged in … what can we call it … a highly-delicate mission … hmm?'

'That's exactly the point, Fabian. The man is toxic. I can give you chapter and verse if you need it. But I'm telling you that McCoig is putting your 'mission' in jeopardy and you should pull him out.'

'Hmm. Hmm. This is very disturbing. *Very* disturbing. May I ask … has something of a *personal* nature occurred to disrupt normal comradely relations between you and this individual? Hmm?'

Fabian was the most obtuse person I knew. But he had his moments.

'No. It's not that. I don't know McCoig and I don't want to. I don't know Hackworth either, but he seems to be the right man for the job. McCoig isn't … do you want the details?'

Time was running short and so was my temper. I didn't have time for Fabian's evasions.

'No, no, no … at least, not at this stage. You've been a trusted member of the Department's local programme for

Cassandra

years … albeit at a fairly low level, if I may put it that way without giving offence …. and it has to be borne in mind that you're in *Prague,* after all … but leave it with me, Ian. I will talk to the powers that be and ask them to take your reservations into account. Is that acceptable to you? Hmm?'

I ended the call. Had Fabian got the message? Possibly. Did Fabian have the clout to make 'the powers that be' pay attention? Doubtful.

I knew what the answer would be and I was right.

No change.

I tried to see things from their point of view. I was someone who set up shell companies and managed bank accounts. What did I know about operational matters?

But it was infuriating. I knew I was right and they were wrong.

Pad Thai

Beaujolais threw himself at me as I opened the door. He was still a puppy but weighed as much as a cannon-ball. I staggered, but couldn't bring myself to chide him. Unalloyed adoration. 'If you want love, get a dog'.

As if to prove the point, Galena was staring balefully at me from the sofa. I leant down to give her a kiss. Her lap was full of page-proofs for an exhibition catalogue, covered in red ink.

'Look at this!' she hissed. 'Just look! It's utter rubbish!'

'Well, I'm very sorry, milacku. Can I do anything?'

'No. Yes. No. Maybe. But we're opening *next week!*' She glared at me as if it were somehow my fault. Was it? How could it be?

'I'd love to help, but … you seem to be blaming me …'

'It's in English!' she rasped.

Ah. So that was it. English was the *lingua franca* of the art world. American, in fact, but there was no point making this distinction to a Czech. *They* had been crushed, robbed and disinherited – first by the Nazis, then by the Soviets – while *we* had been comfortably spreading our cultural dominion over the entire world. There was nothing I could say, so I went into the kitchen.

Beaujolais came with me. He was hungry. He was, after all, *my* dog and it was *my* responsibility to feed him. So I did. Then … yes, Pad Thai. That should put a smile back on Galena's face.

I cut two chicken breasts in strips and set them to marinate in dark soy, brown sugar and lemon juice. Then the sauce: light soy, a splash of rice wine, chopped garlic, spring onions in slivers, a dash of cumin, shredded ginger, a sliced green chilli … what had I forgotten? I scanned the shelves. Oh

Pad Thai

yes … Next, the veg. A green pepper and a shallot. Thinly-sliced carrots. Some runner beans. Then I put the noodles on.

Thirty minutes later we sat down to eat. Beaujolais arranged himself over my feet. He was happy. More to the point, so was Galena. She was ready for conversation.

'Don't forget the *vernissage* on Tuesday evening.'

'How could I forget? But remind me – I've had a lot on my mind – what's the exhibition about?'

A withering look.

'Oppression! That's why it's called 'A Cry for Freedom', or had you forgotten that, too? We're showing paintings, photographs and sculptures from artists working in impossible conditions … Iran, Palestine, Yemen, Burma, Scotland …'

'*Scotland?*'

'Yes. Of course. A small country crushed under the heel of its larger neighbour, poverty-stricken and deprived of opportunity, subject to ethnic disadvantage enshrined in the exploitative…'

'But hang on a minute! *I'm* from Scotland! It's nothing like that!'

'There's a Quisling clique in every occupied territory' she said, looking down at her plate. 'They work hand-in-glove with the alien power, making sure that their families monopolise the best opportunities, the best jobs, the best education …'

'But just a minute!' I spluttered. 'Are you suggesting this applies to me? My dad was a welder, for goodness' sake. I went to Lanark Grammar!'

Galena raised her eyebrows. I was refusing to fit her ideological model, and that must also be my fault. She had nothing more to say on the subject.

Perhaps Galena was confusing my modest success in film production with a life of privilege. From her point of view, I

Pad Thai

had a decent income, a nice apartment and a car that wasn't a Skoda. It suited her, somehow, to see me as born with a silver spoon in my mouth while my compatriots lived on porridge and dressed in rags.

I realised something else. This relationship was on its last legs. Damn! I should have seen it coming. I should have paid more attention. Who would make the first, or last, move? I thought about damage limitation. I was 45 and I'd been this way before, so I ought to know what I was doing.

But did I? I'd been very smitten by Galena. She looked good, she was smart and ambitious. Like a lot of Czech women, she was making her own way in a world which was new, exciting and full of opportunity. It was also full of dangers, but none of them seemed to care about that. The communist cocoon they'd grown up in had collapsed overnight and some very bad actors – people like Sokol - had seized the advantage. Very few were oligarchs. Most of them were just chancers and con-men. But they shared the same morals. 'If you're not stealing from the state you're stealing from your family.'

Galena knew a lot about art and had strong, emotional opinions about everything under the sun. I had never seen her mask her feelings. Very un-English. Very, very un-Scottish. Exciting, to someone raised in Lanark. And now her sentiments towards me were becoming clear: I was annoying her. I was probably boring her. She could do better. Time to move on. Ah, well.

I leant back in my chair. Beaujolais groaned. At least *someone* understood me.

Dragunov

Hackworth wanted to thank me for his visit to Barrandov. He'd discovered that you can shoot interesting weapons at Czech rifle-ranges and he'd booked us a session.

We drove up the E65 towards Mlada Boleslav. 'Turn off here'. We followed a winding road through pine-trees and came to a military training area left over from the Soviet era.

It was vast. On all sides were barracks and hangars slowly falling into ruin. Concrete, asbestos and galvanized iron. None of it had been built to last. Thrown up in a hurry, abandoned in a hurry, the whole site was a picture of neglect.

We were getting close and Hackworth was excited. I began to wonder if this visit was for my benefit or his. I'd done a bit of shooting at school – there was no option in the cadet force – but nothing since. I was wary of anything to do with guns, but for Hackworth they were presumably the tools of his trade.

We arrived at a compound with a gate, a gatehouse and two guards in combat gear. Hackworth produced our booking documents and we were told, in perfect English: 'Welcome to Puska Point! Please go along the track until you see the range-buildings. One of my colleagues will greet you there.' He turned to mutter into his two-way radio.

I parked and we got out. It was a perfect day for shooting – clear, cool but sunny, with hardly a breath of wind. The air was laden with the scent of pine-resin.

We were invited into the briefing-room and given a half-hour lecture on gun safety. Hackworth looked bored but I'd never heard anything like this before – certainly not at school. It seemed that everything from now on would be timed, organized and controlled to the letter. We were in the hands of professionals.

Dragunov

We were taken into an adjoining room and kitted out with denim fatigues, name-tags and ear-protectors. 'Are you right-handed or left?' We were both right-handed and were given one left-hand glove each.

We'd be firing three kinds of weapon today. First a CR 75 pistol, then a Kalashnikov AK 47 ('everybody's favourite', said our instructor), and lastly a Dragunov SVD 63 sniper-rifle. We walked across to the first firing-station, a shelter with a long table, a couple of chairs and a view of two very small targets 25 metres away.

As we approached I heard a voice. 'Ian! Long time no see!' It was Antonin, the owner. He'd been a captain in the Swiss Army and came to Czechoslovakia in 1990, buying up a fleet of surplus tanks from the Československá armáda. Antonin made a good living by renting them to film companies and I'd met him several times on location.

'I didn't have you down as a small-arms type!' he said.

'I'm not really. I'm here as the guest of my friend Adrian.' They shook hands.

'Well, must press on. Have a good time! And Adrian – just make sure Ian's facing the right way!'

We were shown how to stand, how to hold the gun, how to aim, how to breathe, how to pull the trigger, and how to put the weapon down safely once our magazines were empty. Hackworth had heard it all before, and let it show.

We stepped forward. The CR 75 was surprisingly heavy. I turned sideways on to my target, squinted through the sights and pulled the trigger as gently as I could. There was a muted 'crack' and the gun leapt in my hand. Beside me Hackworth was blazing away like a video-game: 'bang-bang-bang-bang-bang-bang.' I was ready for my second shot.

Dragunov

I breathed out, as instructed, and brought the sights down slowly onto the centre of the target. 'Crack'. Then I paused for another breath. Rinse and repeat. After six shots I put the gun down carefully on the table.

'I'm guessing that you haven't done much shooting before?' said the instructor, Jiri. I admitted what was obvious. 'But you, Sir, seem to be an old hand?' Hackworth smiled complacently.

We had to wait a few minutes until firing on the other ranges stopped, then a bell sounded. We walked down to look at our results.

Hackworth had done well with his fast-and-furious fusillade. There were four shots in the black, one in the white and one nowhere. 'Very good!' said Jiri. Hackworth had expected nothing else.

Then we crossed over to look at mine. There was a big hole in the middle of the target and three holes in the white area outside it. 'I'm not sure what's happened here'. Jiri took a closer look. So did Hackworth.

'Well, unless I'm very much mistaken, you've put three shots through the ten and missed altogether with the other three. We don't see that very often. Are you *sure* you haven't done this before?'

'There must be some mistake,' I said.

'No ... if you look here you'll see ... two there, overlapping, and one there. That's really quite good.'

It was embarrassing. Hackworth was giving me a funny look. 'Oh, well – beginner's luck, or something like that.' I laughed it off.

We moved on to the Kalashnikov stand. This Russian semi-automatic was an icon. Hackworth knew all about it. 'Can you believe that over 100 million of these have been

Dragunov

made?' I could. You saw them whenever you turned on the TV news.

We were given a detailed briefing and I tried to pay attention, but I was remembering *'Naming of Parts'* by Henry Reed.

We were told that the idea was to fire short, three-round bursts. 'Some of the young chaps from England empty the whole magazine in one go!' said Jiri. 'Absolutely pointless in battle-conditions. It's not a machine-gun!'

Of course not.

We stepped forward and picked up our weapons. We were firing from the shoulder, standing. I got into position and looked down the sights at the target 50 metres away. It seemed a lot easier to line up the bullseye with an AK 47. But what did I know? I squeezed the trigger briefly.

The gun kicked slightly and I felt a mild recoil in my shoulder, but nothing like what I'd been expecting. Maybe this was the secret of the Kalashnikov's popularity.

I lifted the barrel and took a breath, then lowered it slowly onto the target and fired another short burst. Then again, and again. I was vaguely aware that Hackworth had emptied his magazine in two bursts, but I was intent on following the instructions.

We waited for the bell and walked down to inspect our targets. We looked at Hackworth's first, since we all seemed to agree that he was the senior person here.

'Huh – not bad at all!' said Jiri. Half Hackworth's target had disappeared, leaving a tattered remnant in the clips.

Then we looked at mine. More accurately, we looked *for* mine. There was nothing there. My target had vanished.

Jiri looked perplexed. 'You've literally blown yours away, Mr McKerrell. I must say – well done! That's exactly what an AK 47 is for.'

Dragunov

Hackworth slapped me on the back, a bit harder than necessary. I put on an expressionless face. I had no idea what was happening, or how.

Time for the Dragunov. I knew a bit about this rifle because Alasdair raved about it whenever we met for a drink. It was like listening to a train-spotter drone on about the virtues of a DB 101, but some of it must have stuck.

It was another Russian masterpiece, nearly as old as the Kalashnikov and still in service all over the world. It could put a round through the eye of a needle at 800 metres. In the right hands. Like all guns it was spare and functional, but there was something special about this one.

We were briefed. This time we'd shoot sitting down, with our elbows resting on the table. The targets were at 200 metres. Jiri told us that complete stillness was the key to success. We had to slow our pulse-rate and control our breathing until we were like lumps of stone. Then squeeze the trigger very, very gently.

I tried this. I imagined I was sitting at my desk with my feet up, totally relaxed, brain in neutral … a fair portrait of my working day.

The Dragunov 'felt right'. It was easy to imagine that this rifle had been designed and built with me in mind. Fanciful, I knew, but when I test-drove a 911 I had exactly the same sensation.

I liked it. I wanted it to do well.

It did. When we walked down to the targets my Dragunov had obliterated the black. Now, at last, I felt proud and ready to look Hackworth in the eye. But he avoided me … he'd got a couple of sevens, a couple of blacks and two off the target altogether.

Dragunov

Jiri was very pleased. 'I don't expect this kind of shooting from the *English*!' he said xenophobically, but with a big grin. 'I want you both to sign your targets for our Hall of Fame'.

'I bet you say that to all the girls!'

We handed in our kit, signed our targets and were given diplomas. We were also given small glasses of Becherovka. 'It's a tradition', said Jiri.

Hackworth sniffed his and made a face. I downed it when Jiri wasn't looking.

As we drove back to Prague I was conscious of Hackworth giving me sidelong looks. He didn't say much, which was not like him.

'OK, Adrian. What's up?' I asked after 20 kilometres.

There was a silence.

'I'm just not sure what to say. I've been practising on the Department's range for years, and I regularly win the annual trophy for side-arms *and* rifles. But here *you* are, with no training or experience whatsoever, getting results that would qualify you as a departmental marksman'.

I can't pretend I wasn't pleased to hear this. In fact, I hugged myself with glee. I was still the driver, but now I felt less like a chauffeur. Even so, I had to make him feel better.

'Don't forget, Adrian, that half the Red Army's best snipers, with over a hundred scalps to their credit, were 18-year-old girls straight out of school.'

That seemed to work.

When I dropped him off he shook my hand warmly, clapped me on the shoulder and said: 'You know, Ian, you're wasted in movie lighting.'

Operation *Can Has*

I got in early and set up a small office for Hackworth and McCoig. They didn't need much – a couple of laptops. Notepads and pens? No. Waste-bin? No. Wall-charts? No. Staplers? No. It was hard to simulate a busy office these days.

A noise in reception told me they'd arrived. Svetlana showed them in.

Svetlana … as tall as me, athletic, striking … not conventionally pretty but a head-turner. Strong features, red hair. She spent her spare time climbing rocks, kayaking and doing martial arts. She was also the heart and soul of the company – everyone's best friend.

I showed Hackworth and McCoig what was where and told them how to operate the coffee-machine in the kitchen. I didn't have much to say, but I needed to go through the motions.

Hackworth settled down at once and fired up his laptop, asking important questions about bandwidth and passcodes. But there was something odd about McCoig.

He couldn't take his eyes off Svetlana. Even odder, she couldn't take her eyes off him.

When Svetlana left the room we got down to business. Maps, Google Earth, distances, timings. If I'd had doubts about getting involved at the 'sharp end' – and I had – they were swept away as my role in Operation *Can Has* became clear.

Hackworth would wear a wetsuit and lurk in the lake while it was still dark. McCoig would hide in the bushes on the bank as back-up. I would conceal the car in a copse and watch out for Sokol's security detail. They were not meant to interfere with his 'wild swimming' but who knew?

Operation Can Has

We had a plan, but - as every soldier knows - no plan survives contact with the enemy. What could go wrong? Anything. We went through every contingency we could think of. Over and over. Sod's Law says that what happens is the one thing you haven't thought of, and we all knew Sod was right.

I went back to my own room to do work that I was paid for. At lunch-time I looked in on my guests. Hackworth was tapping away and gave me a cheerful grin. I left him to it and went out for a snack. On the way back I spotted Svetlana and McCoig through the window of a small restaurant in Betlemske namesti. There was a bottle of Barolo between them and they were staring into each others' eyes. *Oh no.*

They didn't see me. I slunk past and returned to the office.

Hackworth had something to tell me. 'I say, Ian. I know we're only pretending to be lighting experts but – look – I've found this great deal on reflectors that I thought you'd want to know about!'

The schoolboy again. It was touching, really - just not what I expected from a cold-blooded killer. But, as I would discover, Hackworth was a complicated creature.

The afternoon dragged by. Svetlana returned to her post in the main office, looking slightly flustered. McCoig returned two minutes later, looking slightly human.

At 4pm Sarka came into my room.

Mid-twenties, clever, hard-working, shy.

'Ian …' she didn't seem to know what to say.

'Yes, Sarka, what is it?'

'Well … it's a bit embarrassing … but … the ladies' loo has been occupied for a long time and … well … some of us need to … use it …'.

I guessed immediately what was going on.

'Sarka – please use the gents' loo for now.'

Operation Can Has

'Oh, but Ian … are you sure? I mean …'

'Yes, Sarka. You and everyone else. Imagine we were in Munich or Paris, and all the facilities were unisex. Would that work for you?'

'Umm … if you're sure … yes, I suppose so.'

Sarka left. I waited for ten minutes, then headed for the toilets. I banged on the door marked 'Zeny'. Nothing. I banged harder, and heard a faint scuffling from within.

'Come on now!' I commanded. 'Out!'

There was a pause, then the door opened a crack. Svetlana's nose appeared.

'Out! Now!'

Svetlana sidled out, squeezing past without looking at me. I pushed the door fully open and there was McCoig, shirt out and hair, what there was of it, all over the place.

I glared at him and for once he looked back at me. He seemed pleased with himself.

What could I say? There was the 'inconvenience' but that wasn't funny in any language. I was more concerned about security. Weren't the Department's operatives supposed to keep their distance from civilians? Was this a breach of procedural rules or just normal practice? I didn't know, but it couldn't be professional and I didn't like it.

I really didn't know, because I had no idea what the Department's operational rules were. But as it turned out I'd hit the nail on the head.

A Phone-call to William

'Yes?'

'Hello - is that William?'

'Who are you?'

'It's Ian at Lanark Lighting'.

'Just a minute'.

There was a pause while his system verified my identity. But it wasn't enough for William.

'Who won the Scottish Cup in 2020?'

'For goodness' sake, William ...'

'All right ... which major golf tournament was originally held at Prestwick in 1860?'

'What is this, William, a pub-quiz? I'm calling you on a professional basis because I want some important operational information!'

'OK. That'll do. Just testing, you know. Only a real person could be that ignorant. Well ... only *some* real people ...'

It wasn't worth getting annoyed. William didn't know what it was to give or take offence. I sometimes wondered how he made it through '*Are You Human?*' filters.

'Right. Is this line secure?'

'Silly question. Next?'

'OK. Thanks. Now – what can you tell me about Stepan Sokol?'

William was a walking Google. In some ways better, because he knew why you were asking. In some ways worse, because he had emotions. Though not many.

'Sokol? He's a bit of a blank, but that's only because he has the media under his thumb. It's all quite boring. He was a mid-level executive in the MoD when everything went up for grabs in 1989, and what he grabbed was a chunk of the Czech

A Phone-call to William

munitions industry. Since then he's been selling everything and anything to everybody and anyone. He's made a lot of money, lives in isolation somewhere near Tabor, has a daughter he dotes on and gives a lot of money to Czech sports teams.'

'Any obvious reason why he should worry NATO?'

'Not really. Too small-scale. But he's not particular about his customers, so you'll find him selling Swedish artillery to the Taliban and Swiss ammunition to insurgents in Chad. He's not fussy.'

'OK ... any reason why he should worry *anyone*?'

'Well, yes. If you're the State Department you don't want some freelance arms dealer providing state-of-the-art anti-aircraft missiles to the enemies of your allies. If you're Israel you don't want someone like Sokol giving Hamas kit you can't procure yourselves.'

Israel? I delved into my thin memory of post-war Middle East history.

'But I thought it was the Czechs who supplied Israel with the weapons they needed to fight off the Arabs in 1948?'

William laughed. 'Yes, but that was then and this is now. We're not talking geopolitics. Sokol's a businessman, pure and simple.'

I got the picture. At least, I thought I did.

It was time for revenge.

'I have a one for *you*. Where is Robert the Bruce buried?'

'Ha! Trick question! Supposedly in Dunfermline Abbey, but no-one's ever found the site of his grave.'

'All right... here's another one. Which Scots player ended up managing Manchester United?'

William groaned. 'Tommy Docherty, of course! *Everyone* knows that!'

'OK ... now: which is the oldest distillery in Scotland?

A Phone-call to William

Probably Glenturret. But some people make a case for Littlemill'.

I gave up. 'Usual fee to Transcendental Activation SRO?'

'Yes. But I'll warn you in advance – my rates are going up in August.'

Most people would have broken this news gently. Perhaps a letter, maybe a drink or even a dinner if the client was important enough. But not William. Take it or leave it. I took it.

'Fair enough.'

There was only one William, and he knew it. My negotiating position wasn't just weak, it didn't exist.

Cloak and Dagger

For all his omniscience, William hadn't told me anything new about the mysterious Mr Sokol. I wanted to know more. Who could I ask without compromising security?

My landlord had lived in Prague for twenty years. He invested in just about everything that made a profit and knew everybody. I thought up a makeshift cover-story and invited him for a drink.

We met at the White Lion. Not my favorite pub, but his. It was very dark inside and it took me a minute to adjust. No music, just the low murmur of conversation between wheelers and dealers like Jason. It was a good pub in a historic building. For some reason he didn't own it.

Jason was already there at a table in the back. He was wearing his usual get-up: Paul Smith, Turnbull & Asser, Ferragamo on his feet. His blond hair had obviously been cut and styled within the last 24 hours.

'Jason – how are things?'

'Pretty good, Ian. The business parks are going great guns and the retail is OK ... though between ourselves I've taken a bit of a beating on foreign exchange.'

'Oh no!' I said sympathetically, having no idea what he meant.

'Yes. I just didn't expect the Czech Crown to stay so strong for so long. Still, you've only got to be right 51 per cent of the time.'

He seemed cheerful enough about it.

'Jason, I need your advice.'

'If you're buying, fire away!'

'It's very much under wraps, if you know what I mean.'

'Ian – I work in property. Of course I know what you mean.'

Of course. I could have made a better start to the conversation. But I carried on.

'As you know, Lanark is only involved in the technical aspects of film production – low risk, low reward.'

'Yes' said Jason. 'That's what I've always liked about your business. Solid, steady income. Good cash-flow. Predictable. Not many surprises. Not much capital tied up. Makes you a good tenant!'

'The thing is, I've been asked to take a slice of the action in a documentary project investigating Czechs who made *real* money from the fall of the communist system. I'm tempted, but I don't know enough about the subject to make an informed decision.'

'So what's the problem? And are your friends looking for more investors?'

I should have seen this coming. Jason was a hard-nosed operator but he had a weakness for anything to do with The Movies. I would have to be careful not to take this too far.

'I don't know. It's early days. Anyway, *my* problem is that I know next to nothing about oligarchs, so can't tell if these guys will be able to get enough material together to make their doco worth watching.'

'I see what you mean. Yes, they all play their cards pretty close to the chest. They like the shadows. And they control the media. You get the occasional rich guy who wants to go into politics … big mistake if you want to keep things discreet. But most of them have more sense.'

'Exactly. So, just to take an example, what do you know about Karl Steiger? All I know is that he's a big wheel in heavy engineering.'

Jason gave me a look.

'Steiger? Keep well away would be my advice. He doesn't mess around. Anyone who gets on the wrong of Steiger lives to regret it. Or, if the word on the street is to be believed, doesn't.'

'Blimey. I thought they were asking me to risk my money, not my life. Well, what about someone like Boris Cerny?'

'He's different. Made a few smart moves in forestry when the state sold off its holdings, then built up a paper products combine which later expanded into glass and plastics. As far as I know, he's a 'normal' businessman, much the same as you'll find in Germany or the UK.'

I was tempted to ask what 'normal' meant when Britain's biggest bank had crashed in flames and VW were still paying out millions for fitting cars with emissions cheat devices. But I let it go.

'OK. So he might be a good *positive* example for the film. We'll need some of those to make sure the content is balanced. How about Tomas Novak of Magenta Superstores?'

'Same story. What you see is what you get. He's done well, no question, but it's all about high-throughput, low margin. A bit like you.' Jason smirked.

I didn't rise to the bait.

'All right… what about someone like Stepan Sokol?'

Jason gave me that look again.

'Remember what I said about Steiger? Double it for Sokol.'

This was what I wanted to know. 'Why? What's he got to hide?'

'Everything. Except his daughter.'

'Meaning?'

'His nickname's 'Semtex'. He makes his money by trading arms to people who shouldn't have them. It's like the cartels.

Outside the law, more or less untouchable, corrupt as hell, viciously competitive. Nasty business. Nasty man.'

'I'm getting the impression that my friends won't have any subjects left apart from a chap who makes kitchen-towel and a supermarket-operator.'

'True' said Johnnie. 'But there's always me!'

That gave me an idea. Perhaps there really *was* a documentary to be made about foreigners who'd swooped into Central Europe after the fall of the Berlin Wall. Nothing nefarious – not much, anyway – but a buccaneering story about opportunities seized and fortunes made.

'There's a thought' I said. 'Tell me, what car are you driving these days?'

Jason looked faintly embarrassed.

'Bentayga' he mumbled.

'And where are you living?'

He looked down at his glass.

'Um ... do you mean here or abroad? We've still got the place in Vinohrady and the farm ... then we've got a pied-a-tierre in Mount Street, as you know ... then Marilyn made me buy a villa in Sardinia – only a small one mind, 800 metres – so the children would have their own place for holidays ... that sort of thing ...'

It was a different world. I wondered how Jason managed to seem so normal. Then I remembered his fits of depression. Jason had his problems and his demons, just like everyone else. But that wasn't the point. He was a classic case of a foreign entrepreneur who'd got rich in Prague.

'You'll do! And how do you feel about wearing mascara?'

Jason looked puzzled, then he saw the point and laughed.

'If Orlando Bloom can do it, so can I!'

Carsten

I was out of my depth. The Department had inveigled me into an operational role, probably in a fit of absent-mindedness. They'd given me no training and no background briefing. I was about to tangle with an arms dealer but I knew little about arms and nothing about dealing.

However, I knew Carsten.

There was no corner of the world of weaponry that Carsten hadn't mastered in intimate detail. He'd spent his long career writing about defence, geo-politics and the military-industrial complex for international news media like the FT and the FAZ. He spoke German, English, Russian and – for all I knew – Swahili.

For Carsten, his media beat wasn't a job but a vocation. You could ask him the exact dimensions of a Fairbairn-Sykes Commando Knife and he'd tell you, off the top of his head. If you wanted to know the effective range of a Varunastra torpedo, he knew. Rate of fire of the Rheinmetall 30mm Mk 30-ABM? Carsten could tell you. Omniscient, like William, but … normal.

These days Carsten lived in a mountainside hideaway near Chamonix and made his living as a consultant. I decided to consult him.

Among Carsten's many idiosyncrasies was a profound love of Czech spa towns. I never knew why, but I knew how to arouse his interest.

'Carsten, how do you fancy a weekend in Karlovy Vary?'

'Very much. But why do you ask?'

'I need your help, and this is the lure.'

'Consider me hooked.'

Carsten

Svetlana reserved a suite for Carsten and Mrs Carsten at the Grandhotel Pupp. They knew Svetlana. She'd booked rooms for our film festival guests for years, so she got a very good rate. I didn't need to tell Carsten.

I wanted an hour of his time, so we met at the Café Pupp for coffee and cakes. I was driving and he didn't drink during the day, so we were happy to risk atherosclerosis – Pupp chocolate cake was the Food of the Gods.

'This is an unexpected pleasure' said Carsten happily. Then he saw my expression. 'Ian – is something wrong?'

'It's hard to explain. May I ask you to keep what I tell you here absolutely confidential?'

Carsten looked pained.

'Of course. Remember what I have done for a living these last thirty years. Apart from which … you are a friend.'

One of the downsides of Scots ancestry is a tendency to blush when embarrassed. This I did.

'I'm sorry … the thing is, I'm getting involved in an area where I don't really know what I'm doing, and it could be risky.'

'Interesting. Tell me more.'

Our coffee arrived with a plate of cakes.

'Carsten, what's your secret vice?'

'Chocolate cakes. Yours?'

'Chocolate cakes.'

We set to.

'I've never mentioned this before, but from time to time I do a bit of low-level stuff for HMG … you know, financial transactions and the like, all below the radar…'

'Ian, I have known this ever since I met you. What's new?'

Carsten took a mouthful of *Pupp's Cake* while enjoying my reaction.

Carsten

'You knew? Really? How?'

'Oh, little things. Don't forget I talk to people like you all the time. It's not so hard to spot the signs … even if they consider themselves 'low-level'. In fact, those are even easier.'

One day I would need to know what had given me away to Carsten, but not now. I wanted information.

'The thing is… I'm about to get embroiled in a plot involving a Czech arms dealer, and I don't know anything about the industry. I want to know how it works, and I thought you'd be the best person to give me *'Arms Dealing for Dummies'*. I put on my rabbit face.

'I suppose it goes without saying that we are discussing *illicit* trading in armaments?'

'Yes.'

'I thought so. When one hears the words 'arms-dealer' and 'Czech' one jumps to certain conclusions.'

'OK. So how does it work?'

Carsten looked at his watch.

'I can give you an overview. If you need more, I am always available for further spa treatments.'

'Yes, please.'

'You are obviously aware that there are numerous governments and insurrectionist movements whose aims are deemed antithetical to the interests of countries who manufacture weapons and munitions?'

'Yes.'

'Let's agree that the best and most advanced weaponry comes from factories in Europe and the United States – though this is less true today than it was twenty years ago.'

'Yes.'

'Now let's imagine that you are a proscribed organization seeking to overthrow a government which the West – let's call it NATO – has decided it wishes to support.'

'I'm with you so far.'

'You need good weapons. You have money. What do you do?'

'I suppose you turn to the 'Black Market'. Is it called that?'

'No, Ian, it isn't. But you're on the right track. You need someone who can get advanced kit from Western manufacturers and deliver it to you in quantity without interference from the authorities who exist to prevent this kind of thing from happening.'

'How do they do it?'

'Money. Pure and simple.'

'But we spend millions – maybe billions – on people and systems to prevent it. You're suggesting that it goes on anyway. How?'

'Ian, imagine that you're a port official on a salary of € 30,000 a year. A pleasant chap comes up to you in a bar and asks you, very politely, to turn a blind eye next Wednesday. He tucks an envelope in your pocket and leaves. When you look, the envelope contains € 10,000.'

'Tempting. But what if you decide to stick to the rules?'

'Your daughter might disappear on her way home from school. Your wife might lose her job for no reason. Your car might go up in flames.'

'It sounds very like the tactics of narcotics traffickers.'

Carsten clapped his hands.

'That's because it is.'

'OK … I think I understand. *Plata o plomo*?'

'Yes. It's illegal, just like drugs, and the exact same techniques apply.'

Carsten

'I had no idea. But why don't the manufacturers put a stop to it?'

'Why should they? They are corporations with shareholders. They want sales. It is not in their interests to look too closely at who they're selling to, and the existence of 'arms-dealers' means they rarely have to.'

'I had no idea! But can't governments clamp down?'

'They can. Sometimes they do. But there's an interesting twist to this story. Do you remember Guatemala and Nicaragua? The CIA? Long story short, the US government paid for secret agents to bring down regimes which it officially supported but covertly detested. This saga happened to hit the media. Most don't.'

'You mean … democratic governments could be guilty of using illicit arms-dealers to supply dissident movements which they secretly support but publicly disavow?'

'Yes. It happens all the time. Don't look so shocked! Or do you imagine that you live in a democracy? Ian, you can't be *that* naïve!'

Carsten had more to say.

'I think you may find this is precisely what's going on between the clandestine organs of your government and people like … just to pick a name at random … Stepan Sokol.'

I nearly fell off my chair. I was aghast. How could he possibly know this? And, if Carsten knew, who else did?

Carsten had finished his cakes. He stood up, patted me on the shoulder and headed off for his spa treatment, grinning broadly.

I felt like a child who's been told that Father Christmas doesn't exist.

Carsten

I left Café Pupp uncertain about many things but sure of two. I would have to buy some more chocolate cakes before long. And I would have to watch my step.

Andelsky Pivovar

It was the third Tuesday in the month, which meant four beers and steak tartare with Ondrej.

He was an independent film producer and one of Lanark's best clients. I'd known him for years and always looked forward to our conversations. Ondrej hoarded information; he kept up with world affairs and had opinions about nearly everything. If he didn't have opinions he had questions.

Ondrej specialized in historical drama and the occasional documentary. He had encyclopaedic knowledge of everything from Thermopylae to the Hurtgen Forest. The only gap was Scotland's turbulent chronicle, and he was even interested in that. Handy for me, because it was the sole subject I could tell him anything about.

Ondrej could have worked wherever he liked. He'd had offer after offer from Hollywood. But like many Czechs he loved his country and didn't want to live anywhere else. As an ex-pat I liked him, and envied him, for this.

He lived in Mala Strana so I walked across Charles Bridge feeling, as always, that I was being watched from the countless windows of the Castle. On either side were the thirty statues of the saints. I felt sorry for them, stuck there on the parapet in all weathers, doomed to grip their croziers and prayerbooks in stony silence, frozen for eternity. I liked to imagine that every so often, when no-one was looking, they jumped down and danced a polka on the cobbles.

We met as usual at the Andelsky Pivovar, a craft brewery not far from the river. I made my way downstairs and paused to look at the vats, pipes, retorts and cylinders in the brewhouse, all in gleaming steel and copper. It gave me a

Andelsky Pivovar

childish thrill to drink beer which I could see being made not three steps away from my chair.

I was first to arrive. I was shown to a table by a smiling waitress and given a menu. Exactly one minute later she was back, still smiling, to take my order.

I asked for two Lezak and started in on mine. It was good.

Ondrej turned up in a whirl five minutes later. 'I'm so sorry to have kept you waiting!'

He wore a puffa jacket, a two-metre scarf and jeans. His long black hair covered half his face. He hadn't shaved for three days. I was used to this. The 'bohemian' look was common in the film industry and Ondrej was an extreme case.

'You haven't. Look!' There was still a head of foam on our glasses.

'Oof. It's been quite a day. I am really sorry to be late.'

Czechs, like Germans, think punctuality is a cardinal virtue.

'Please! Sit down. Relax. Have a drink.' We clinked glasses. 'Na zdravi!'

We talked about movies that had been made, were being made, could have been made, should not have been made, were due to be made and would never be made. We talked about the effect of AGI on screenplays. Then we talked about Ondrej's new daughter. He showed me her latest pictures on his phone. Then he asked me about Celtic and Rangers.

'Do you want the thirty-minute lecture or the abbreviated version?'

'Which costs more?'

'The short one, of course!'

Then we talked about Russia (we shook our heads) and the United States (same). We talked about his summer holiday in Hvar. The problems of taking a baby on a twelve-hour car journey. Then we talked about the Regia Marina's submarine

Andelsky Pivovar

pens from World War Two, bored out beneath the Croatian cliffs and still there to this day. I had seen them. Ondrej wanted to make a film about them. We discussed the difficulties of lighting these subterranean hideouts, and € signs appeared before my eyes.

The usual topics. But I had a hidden purpose in mind.

'Ondrej … who would you say are the murkiest oligarchs in the Czech Republic?'

He looked surprised. 'That's an odd question. Why – are you looking for investors?'

'No, nothing like that. It's just that some of my clients get funding from – what can I call them? – obscure sources … I just wonder, sometimes, if we might get in trouble with the authorities … if … you know… anyone chose to put one of Lanark's clients through the mill …'

'Yes, I see. I have the same problem myself, obviously. To be honest, I don't look too closely. I can't afford to. If I did 'due diligence' on my investors I wouldn't make a minute of footage.'

'Anyway … off the cuff … who would you say are the worst of the worst?'

'Cuff?'

'Sorry. Slang. It just means 'off the top of your head' … what springs to mind.'

Ondrej smiled. He liked the endless variety of English synonyms and paraphrases. No other language had them, and no other culture needed them.

'Well … *off the cuff*, I would have to say Stepan Sokol.'

'Sokol? I think I've heard of him. Isn't he something to do with horses?'

'No. That's his daughter. Sokol himself is an arms-dealer.'

'Is that bad? If the world was a better place we wouldn't need them, but it isn't, so we do.'

'He's not the government. He's private enterprise. A profiteer.'

'But so is Raytheon. So is Lockheed Martin. What's wrong with Sokol?'

'Hmm'. Ondrej took a long drink. I waved for two more.

'OK. From what I've heard – and bear in mind, it's just what I've heard – his legitimate business only accounts for a small fraction of what he actually does.'

'I'm not sure I follow.'

'Follow …?'

'It just means understand.'

'Oh. OK.' Ondrej was making another mental note.

'What I mean is … he sells weapons, munitions, armaments … whatever you call them … to some very unsavoury customers.'

Ondrej smiled broadly. He knew that 'unsavoury' was the *mot juste*.

'Ahah … I see. So … let's just say that Sokol was financing one of my clients' productions … you'd advise me to be careful?'

'Yes, I would. This would never happen with one of my projects. He is someone I would avoid with a punt-stick.'

For a moment I was confused. 'Oh – a barge-pole!'

'Yes. A *barge-pole*. A long one.'

We went on to talk of other things. Fighter-aircraft, neo-lithic cave-paintings, hip-hop as an art-form, why vinyl was so popular and what it might mean for sound-track recording… whether pigs have wings.

Andelsky Pivovar

When we went upstairs to the street and parted company (Ondrej to the tram, me to Liftago) I shook his hand warmly and thanked him for an enjoyable evening.

But I couldn't thank him for what mattered most – what he'd told me, *off the cuff*, about Stepan Sokol.

The Vernissage

I walked through Old Town Square, past the Clock and its usual crowd of clock-watchers, then made my way across Male namesti. The entrance to Galena's gallery was lit by an array of candles.

I pushed open the door and entered a monochrome world.

Everyone was wearing black. Galena was wearing black. The waiters and waitresses were wearing black. I was wearing black: in my case it was the safety option. Andrew was wearing a nifty black suit from Armani.

The walls had been hung with black sheets. Someone had arranged spots and diffusers to illuminate the pictures, just enough to be visible, while leaving most of the gallery in darkness. The effect was eerie. It was very well done. I would have to get the name of the lighting technician. *Fool!* It was Andrew, of course.

I looked around. It was Dante for the 21st century. Bodies and parts of bodies rendered in paint, charcoal and photographs. Ruined people in ruined buildings. It was gruesome. Would anyone buy these things? I glanced at the guests through the gloom. Grim faces. But the art market in Prague was driven by fashion, not art.

Galena swanned up and grabbed my arm. 'Ian! You're here! Just in time! I want you to meet the Sokols!'

I was dragged through the crowd and hauled into a small circle who were looking at a life-sized painting of a corpse buried in rubble.

'Stepan – Katerina – can I introduce Ian, my partner in crime?'

I was looking at a middle-aged man of middle height, hair carefully arranged to hide incipient baldness, wearing a tailored

The Vernissage

suit which was nearly black but not quite. His features were instantly forgettable. He looked exactly like the mid-level civil servant he once was.

We shook hands. 'And this is my daughter, Katerina.'

She was about nineteen, taller than him, obviously an athlete, wearing a dark-grey trouser suit which said 'Chanel', even to me. Her hair was tied back in a chignon which said 'equestrienne'. We shook hands. Her fingers were slender but her grip was firm and strong.

We all smiled politely at each other.

I needed to say something. 'So … what are your impressions of the pictures?'

Katerina answered: 'It is terrible, awful, dreadful. We see here what happens to ordinary human beings when modern weapons are used to destroy their homes, their lives and their loved ones. It is just terrible. Terrible.'

I guessed she had no idea how her father earned his living, or what was paying for her horses, stables, and hay.

'And what do *you* think of these works, *pane* Sokol?'

He looked me in the face, then his gaze shifted past me. 'Katerina is absolutely right. These pictures show us the real casualties of war. The common people, workers, farmers and so on … they are the true victims, though we never notice them.'

He looked back at me. There was no trace of hypocrisy. His eyes were blue, clear, candid. Was it possible? Then I thought of the Nuremberg Trials. Yes, it was possible.

'I hope we will all learn a lesson from this exhibition' I said, lamely.

'That's the whole point, darling!' It was Galena, eager to drive home her political message, and maybe her commercial

The Vernissage

message too. 'We need to be made aware of the tragic human consequences that are all too easily brushed under the carpet!'

I was about to say something about Lee Miller and Robert Capa, but my moment had passed. Galena was shepherding the Sokols on to talk to another group of influential customers.

But I'd had a clever idea. William said that Sokol doted on his daughter. From what I'd seen this evening it was all that and more … she appeared to be the light of his life. I needed to speak to Fabian, urgently.

My Clever Idea

My Clever Idea

Ring-ring. Ring-ring. Squeak … buzz …. hiss … tick, tick … blurgghh … click.

'Hello? Is that Mr Richards? This is Mr Watts.'

'Yes, Richards here. But surely, Ian, you know by now that once the system has, as it were, ascertained the security of the line by technical means, there is no further need for pseudonyms? We're not dropping agents into occupied France, ha ha ha , don't you know? Hmm?'

'Yes. OK. I take it that I can speak plainly?'

'By all means, by all means. Though I must say that I am a little surprised to hear from you at this, how can I put it, *late juncture*.'

'Yes, Fabian. I expect you are. But I've had an idea which could make everything much less difficult and – as it were – *(I could do this too)* – much less messy.'

'Hmm? Hmm. Well, then, I ought to hear it in order that it can be given due and proper consideration by the higher powers who guide our fates and determine our fortunes. *As it were.* Hmm?'

'Let me lay it on the line. I've got two operatives in my office who are due to murder Stepan Sokol at his estate near Tabor this week.'

'Ian, Ian … this all sounds *far* too explicit. Could we just agree, for the purposes of this discussion, that it may well be that certain events may *possibly* occur in a place not a million miles from South Bohemia which may *possibly* involve a certain person who, for the purposes of this conversation, may not be named but who …'

I couldn't stand this nonsense any longer.

'Fabian! Please! I have a much better idea to put forward!'

My Clever Idea

'Oh. Oh. Hmm. An idea? Really? Well … what is it?'

'Sokol only cares about one thing in life. His daughter, Katerina. We don't need to kill him. We just need to kidnap Katerina and tell him that he stops selling weapons to Hezbollah or he never sees her alive again.'

There was a long silence.

'Fabian?'

'Hmm. Your idea has a certain appeal, it has to be said … it would, for example, preclude the possibility of – what can I call them? – unwelcome after-effects in the event of certain contingencies … and it would have the distinct advantage of deniability on all sides … hmm … let me think, Ian, and let me consult with higher levels. I congratulate you – if I may – even though, as I understand it, you are in fact a *facility* rather than a planning or an operational member of the Department's personnel? Hmm?'

Typical Fabian. He'd acknowledged that my idea was good. I knew it was. At the same time he'd put me in my place. I felt like a corporal who'd had the temerity to make a suggestion to a second lieutenant, exactly as Fabian had intended.

I waited. Two hours, three hours, four hours.

The answer came back by Departmental email.

'Alternative rejected. Original plan to be adhered to in all respects.'

Were they just stupid? Or what? I decided to push back.

'Desired effect can be achieved without bloodshed or after-effects by means of the suggested simple plan. Why not authorized?

Thirty minutes later I got my reply.

'Alternative proposal considered at highest level but rejected on grounds which Prague facility deemed incapable of taking into account.'

My Clever Idea

OK. I was being put back in my box. They were telling me that the reasons for the assassination were above my pay-grade, and – for all I knew – above theirs.

I was consumed with doubts. If we could neutralise Sokol with a simple kidnapping, why wouldn't we? It would be so much easier. But someone, somewhere, wanted him dead. Who and why?

I needed advice.

Not a Welder

Ryanair to Edinburgh, train to Lanark, then a walk to the stone house overlooking the Clyde where I'd grown up. It was mild for Scotland, for the time of year. In other words just above freezing.

My dad met me in the street with Nutcase, the Irish Setter. They'd been for a swift one at the William Wallace. My dad was a dog-lover.

'How's Beaujolais?' were his first words. Before I could answer, Nutcase scented dog on my clothes and jumped up with a yelp. On his hind legs he was as tall as I was.

'Can you ... control him?' I bleated.

'Och, now, he's just being friendly. Happy to see you again.'

Nutcase had never seen me before in his life. But I knew from long experience this was not a discussion worth having.

We went into the house. It was my mam's birthday, which meant it was my annual visit to that strange part of Scotland, north of Hadrian's Wall but south of the Antonine, which her Inverness family looked at down their noses.

She came up for a formal kiss (Inverness) and appraised me.

'You've put on a few pounds since last year, if I'm not mistaken.'

It was always like this. Once I'd passed the medical inspection we could sit down and catch up on family news. My sister was in New York and my brother lived in Singapore. Both were online 25 hours a day, but it pleased my parents to imagine that I knew nothing about my family apart from what they told me themselves.

'I've brought you something very typical from Prague for your birthday.'

She was pleased. Even Highland women like presents.

Not a Welder

She'd made a terrific dinner. Another kilo at least. If I still lived in Lanark I'd be the size of a bus, and I wouldn't have minded a bit. Had the three of us left Scotland to get away from something, or were we just following in the footsteps of the Highlanders who'd sailed off to populate the planet from Pittsburgh to Parattah?

Dinner over, my dad said 'Fancy a pint?'

I'd told Galena he was a welder, but he was actually a manager in the NHS. I couldn't admit that to her. Or to anyone, these days.

The William Wallace wasn't crowded. There were the regulars, like my dad, with their assigned tables and chairs. Then there was a younger crowd standing at the bar. It must have been for their benefit that we could hear Runrig at low volume. I tried not to listen. One wall was covered with team pictures of Third Lanark AC. Defunct since 1967. But if you call your pub 'William Wallace', why not?

I waited for the usual diatribe about 'real beer' and 'that thin stuff you drink in Prague.' I wasn't disappointed. Truth to tell, it was a bit of a treat to get my hands on a pint of old-fashioned ale. There was no point telling my dad that more than half the beer drunk in Scotland was lager – a pallid version of what the Czechs had been perfecting for a thousand years. He wouldn't listen. He was a patriot.

But I had a question. My dad had worked in a large organization all his life. He must have come up against a dilemma like mine, surely?

'Dad ... what do you do when you get instructions that you *know* are wrong, mad, stupid ... you tell them so ... and they ignore you?'

Not a Welder

He gave me a look. 'How can that happen in the lighting business? If you don't like what they want you can just decline the work, can't you?'

He was no fool. But he hadn't a clue what I'd been doing for the Department. Or had he? Could I have given the game away inadvertently?

'Well … just suppose … of course, I'm asking for a friend.'

He gave me another look. He knew I was bluffing but he was my father, I was his son, and his role in life had always been to hand out good advice. It didn't matter if it was taken as long as it was given.

'In the hypothetical circumstances which you describe – on behalf of your friend – I would say that any employer who refuses to see reason is not an employer worth working for. Your own judgement, or moral compass, or whatever you call it, must *always* take precedence over your desire to conform. Even when it means hardship.'

Edict delivered, he got up to fetch another round while I patted Nutcase, who'd finally realised that I wasn't a dog.

'Of course, it depends very much on the circumstances.' He'd had time to reflect while waiting at the bar.

'Let's imagine – just for the sake of argument, you understand – that your friend is involved in some kind of military operation, or something of that nature. Semi-military, let's say. Then it might be a different matter. A very different matter.'

'How do you mean?'

'You've been to the Somme. You know what happened there. 20,000 British soldiers dead – young men, most of them – slaughtered by shells and machine-guns in a single morning. And you know why?'

'Not really. Go on.'

Not a Welder

'Because their orders were – what did you say? – wrong, mad, stupid. Some of them knew that. Some of them argued, but they were told to be silent and do their duty. So they did.'

I wasn't certain what he was telling me. Did he mean that military operations required a different standard of obedience, regardless of personal qualms? Did he mean that *'Dulcis Pro Patria Mori'* was right?

'Do you mean soldiers sign away the right to apply their own moral judgement when they're given orders? Just because they're soldiers?'

'I'm not at all sure they *should*. But that's exactly what they do.'

My mam was pleased with her Moser goblet. She wasn't a drinker (Inverness) but said it would be 'very nice for lemonade in the garden in the summer'. The short, hot Lanarkshire summer.

We were supposed to have four seasons but I'd only ever been aware of two: winter and summer, with brief intermissions that people in England called spring and autumn.

No wonder I felt at home in the Czech Republic.

I left the next day. My parents had been pleased to see me but were happy to wave good-bye for another year. Nutcase was heartbroken. He'd get over it. When you're a dog, anyone will do.

I thought about what my dad had said. He seemed to be making a distinction between 'military' and 'civilian' life when it came to obeying orders. Could that be true?

It probably had to be. There are no jobs in Civvy Street where people are routinely instructed to risk their lives. Police, Fire Service…? Yes, but these are almost para-military organisations run very much like the Army. It can't be a coincidence that so many ex-servicemen join them.

Not a Welder

I ruminated. It was clearly true that different demands were imposed on civilian workers and members of the armed services. Though the rewards seemed to be inverted, for some reason. But this principle could be taken to an extreme – the Wehrmacht in Russia, the SS in Lidice, Oradour – so where should you draw the line?

There had to be a tipping-point somewhere, but for the life of me I couldn't tell what it was or how to identify it.

I needed a second opinion.

A Second Opinion

Father Dominic saw my look as soon as I entered his attic room. He poured the whisky straight away.

'Oh, what can ail thee, knight at arms?' He handed me my glass.

I knew he knew, somehow, but I had to explain it anyway.

'Father Dominic ... what's the right thing to do when you know that your superiors have made a completely wrong decision?'

He took a sip and leant back in his moth-eaten chair.

'It's tricky. I'll give you that. Now, tell me, how familiar are you with the idea of such a thing as a *higher cause*?'

I said I'd heard of it and thought I knew what it meant.

'So ... let me give you a for-instance. Imagine you are a Northern French baron in 1209 AD. You are told that a heresy in Provence threatens the existence of the Church, which – to you – is your sole hope of escaping the fires of hell and attaining the life everlasting'

'Well ...' I began to say. But he continued.

'This isn't just a theoretical idea, Ian. You live in the 13th century and you believe absolutely and without reservation that the Church is your one and only chance of salvation. That's exactly what people thought in the Middle Ages. They *really did*. That's why they paid fortunes to set up chantries and have marble effigies carved for their tombs ... they had no doubt at all that what the Church told them was the *absolute truth*.'

He took another sip. 'Things have changed, of course ...'

'Now. Imagine that you are told – by the Church – to ride south with your men-at-arms and kill every living soul – man, woman, child — that you can find in the territory of the Albigensian heretics. What will you do?'

'I will do what I am told ...?' I ventured.

'Exactly. You may feel in your heart that slashing the head off a five-year-old is wrong ... of course it is ... but you have been told that you *must* do it because it is right. You don't hesitate, and neither did they in 1209. They surrendered their personal judgement to a *higher power*.'

'But that's like saying the Nazi extermination-camp guards were *also* just acting in accordance with their instructions. 'Befehl ist Befehl' and suchlike nonsense! *That* was their pathetic excuse! Utter bullshit! Oh — sorry, Father.'

'Precisely. We could talk for hours — and often have — about the ways in which Holy Mother Church has inadvertently contributed to human misery. I remember we went at it hammer-and-tongs about the Inquisition. But the fact remains, as it always has: human beings are inclined to abandon their own ideas when they feel they are part of a bigger, grander, more important movement. It could be the Albigensian Crusade, it could be Arsenal FC, it could be the Nazi Party. You notice I put these three on the same moral level?'

I had noticed. Father Dominic was a Chelsea supporter. This was not the only reason I sometimes wondered about the reality of his vocation. To say nothing of divine guidance.

'I think it's clear. When you give your loyalty to a larger organization you are committing yourself to a *higher cause*. Your own feelings or scruples are set aside. You hope and trust that it's the route to heaven. You don't *know*. You cannot know. It's entirely a matter of faith'

Father Dominic had answered my question.

'Have I answered your question?'

I nodded.

A Second Opinion

'Now, about young Andrew. I've been thinking ... maybe a more practical course of tuition – for instance, the economic precepts of Milton Friedman – might be more up his street? And yours?' He raised his eyebrows hopefully.

I shrugged, thanked him and left.

Was the Department a 'higher cause?'

It probably was. It stood for the protection of my country and everyone who lived in it, maybe all the more purposeful for being unseen and unrecognized. But did I really need a 'higher cause'?

I probably did. I had no children. I had no religious beliefs. Like everyone else I knew, I wanted the world to be a better place and gave money to charities who said they could achieve this on my behalf ... but I felt a vague need to do more. Perhaps the bits and pieces I had been doing for the Department were my way of satisfying that urge.

I thought of Father Dominic's medieval analogy. Had human nature changed in 800 years? We wore different clothes but we seemed to be doing exactly the same things, some sublime but mostly not. Father Dominic was telling me that I would have to accept the instructions of the Department, even when I didn't like them and felt I knew better.

What he said made sense in a world of absolutes. My parents were comfortable with the idea of Papal Infallibility. It was a cornerstone of their faith, and for all I knew it was the doctrine which gave their belief its meaning and purpose. But it didn't work for me; I'd been educated (so to speak) to regard every 'Great Truth' as provisional, whether it was Einstein's Theory of Relativity or Darwin's Theory of Evolution by Natural Selection.

But then I thought about what Father Dominic was saying. Did he mean that the *actual* truth of religions and scientific

A Second Opinion

hypotheses was irrelevant? That loyalty and belief were their own reward? Was he suggesting that I needed to believe completely in *something*, purely in order to invest my life with purpose? Was this what he meant when he talked about a 'higher cause'?

It was confusing, but Father Dominic had laid it on the line. As always. He thought of me as a lost soul and was certain it would be better for me to give my absolute loyalty to *something* rather than *nothing*. He had his own reasons for advocating this philosophy, but could it be true? I certainly *could* become a hard-core, unflinching servant of the Department, ignoring my doubts about the wisdom and ability of my superiors.

Or… I could strike out on my own and plant trees. I could devote my remaining years to saving the elephant shrew. I could feel virtuous by doing my bit to save the planet and everyone on it.

But I dimly knew my capacities and limitations. I realised that my best chance of serving a 'higher cause' was to work with what I had: the British SIS in Prague. Father Dominic was correct. *'My Department, right or wrong.'*

Katerina

I popped in for a quick one at the Mandarin Oriental.

I liked this hotel, tucked away behind its high enclosure near the Maltese Square and its Lennon Wall. It used to be a monastery and still retains something of the atmosphere. Even when busy it was quiet.

Sitting at the bar, obviously waiting for someone, was Katerina Sokol. She wore a trouser-suit again, but a different one. Prada? Versace? Galena would know.

I caught her eye and expected her to look away, but she didn't She got up and held out her hand.

'Mr Mackerel! How nice to see you again.'

It would have been ungallant to correct her. Anyway, lots of Czechs were called 'fish'.

'The pleasure is all mine, Madame.'

'Please join me, if you have time. I'm meeting my stable-manager in fifteen minutes but I got here early.'

Big smile. I sat down and wondered what the attraction was. Could it be my dapper good looks and suave charm? No …

'Daddy says you work in films!'

'Well, yes … in a modest way. We do the lighting for some of the movies made here in the city and up at Barrandov.'

'How exciting! I've always *loved* the cinema. How *marvellous* to actually work with famous actors and directors *every day*! I'm so envious!'

What was it about movies that reduced grown-ups like Katerina, Jason and Hackworth to saucer-eyed children? I just couldn't fathom it, but then – as she said – I was seeing it every day in all its prosaic tedium. For my money, the really clever stuff was the work of all the people (literally) behind the scenes.

But the studios knew what they were doing, and what they were doing was brilliant PR, decade after decade.

'Well, it all depends. For instance, I'm awestruck when I see you and Kapitan clear a two-metre jump as if it was a pencil. I have no idea how it's done, but it looks fantastic.'

She coloured, and I realized how young she was. Not grown-up at all.

'Oh, it's just practice. And having a good horse. I'm so lucky to have Kapitan. You do realise, don't you, that's it all him and not me?'

I didn't believe this for a second. I thought horses were elegant creatures but stupid and evil-natured. They didn't like me either.

I saw an opportunity to continue my research.

'And your father – *pane* Sokol – does he share your fascination with the world of The Silver Screen?'

She hesitated for a moment, and I took the opportunity to order two more drinks. Hers was a Mimosa.

'Not really' she said at last. 'He's always working, working, working, dawn to dusk. He just doesn't have time for leisure, least of all films.'

She looked sad.

'But he's clearly taken the time to encourage your talent for riding, if that's the right word. The beautiful stables, the meadows, the paddocks, the… I don't really know what I'm talking about!'

She smiled.

'Not many people do, and why should they? But all that's really my mother. She's the driving face, as I believe you say.'

I didn't correct her. I also didn't know that there was such a person.

'Your *mother*?'

Katerina

'Yes. She was the Slovak Three-day Event Champion four years in a row!'

Katerina glowed with pride.

'I see. Well, I know a bit, in a small way, about having a strong mother pushing you along ... if you're anything like me, you grumble when you're young and then realise a lot later how much you owe them.'

'Exactly!' Her face lit up. 'It seemed like slave-driving when I was nine or ten. But I was so lucky. I always loved horses. So strong, so beautiful, so intelligent ...'

I kept my face blank.

'And so fast! So powerful! I loved it, loved it. So my mother didn't have to whip me very hard!'

Then she frowned.

'But I didn't think English mothers were like that.'

'I wouldn't know. I'm not English. I'm from Scotland.'

'But isn't it the same ...'

She saw my expression and broke off.

'A lot of people think that. But no, it's a separate country and always has been. Different language, different customs, different heritage, different everything. We just have a border in common.'

'Oh ... I hope I haven't offended you.'

'Of course not. How could you know? But it would be like someone from Texas thinking you were Russian.'

She recoiled in horror.

'Oh no ... I *have* offended you!'

She was Czech, and knew how to make up for her *faux pas*. Hers was another Mimosa, mine a Macallan.

A few minutes later her stable manager arrived – not, as I'd expected, a stocky rural yeoman but a tall and eye-catching

Katerina

blonde. I shook hands with Katerina and said yes, I would take her on a tour of the studios whenever she had a morning free.

What had I learnt?

I'd assumed that Katerina and her father were very close, but this was not the impression she gave me this evening. I'd imagined that it was Stepan Sokol who poured time and energy into her equestrian career, but no, it was her mother all along.

Then I wondered why they'd turned up at Galena's *vernissage* together, and why he'd seemed so proud and possessive. At the time I saw him as a typical doting father. Now I wasn't so sure. Was Katerina some kind of symbol? A possession? The human equivalent of a Maserati?

If so, it was yet another reason to dislike him.

I'd been fretting about the effect that Sokol's tragic demise would have on his nearest and dearest. I'd had misgivings once I'd seen the pair of them arm-in-arm at Galena's gallery. I'd quelled such thoughts with *'the higher cause'* in mind.

But what if Sokol and his daughter weren't so close after all? Did it let me off the hook, or was that just wishful thinking?

I didn't know, but I began wondering about the plight of children born to monsters. I thought of M A Bormann, son of the head of the Nazi Party Chancellery, who became a missionary. People said it was a life-long act of atonement, but who really knew? What if he'd been a decent human being anyway? Were the sins of the fathers *really* visited upon their sons and daughters until the third or fourth generation?

Either way, I liked Katerina and felt bad about what lay in store for her.

Andrew. I Make a Mistake

The department had its work to do and I had mine.

Andrew came into my room with his laptop open. He was a digital native – in other words, under forty – and could type quicker than he could speak.

'Morning, guv'.

'Morning, Andrew'. I stared at him. He'd been a soldier but wanted to be an actor. He had talent, no question, and he had the looks. He'd plodded through the long trek of auditions, bit-parts, rejections, disappointments and then – like thousands of others – moved sideways. In his case into stage management and then on to lighting, where he was a true star.

Now he was playing the part of a competent, ambitious lighting company manager and he played it to perfection. Andrew was the future of Lanark Lighting. We both knew it.

'I just wanted to check these prices for Gideon's commercial – 'Buy One and Stop Me' – you know, the condom thing.'

We'd landed this lighting contract without a competitive bid. Gideon and I went back a long way.

Andrew ploughed on through the details of costs and mark-ups. As usual, his draft was perfect. He didn't need advice but he wanted my seal of approval.

He asked: 'The one thing that worries me is that we're making a small margin on so many bits and pieces of equipment. Wouldn't we do better with some kind of package contract?'

He was definitely right, but I had something to contribute. 'Well, Andrew, don't forget what we say on the Clyde: many a mickle makes a muckle!'

'What?'

I let it go.

Andrew. I Make a Mistake

'By the way, Andrew – I hope you're free to attend Galena's *vernissage* on Tuesday? It would mean a lot to us both if you could be there.'

Andrew looked embarrassed. 'Of course, guv – it's been in my calendar for weeks.'

I congratulated Andrew on his work and off he went.

I began to wonder. Was it possible …? No, surely not. But then … what could account for Galena's hostility over the past few weeks? Had I changed? I didn't think so. Had *she* changed? Yes, or so it seemed to me. What could account for it? Could it be … no, that was a crazy idea. *You're being paranoid!*

Or was I? suddenly things began to fall into place. A few odd coincidences that meant nothing at the time, but now … . I wasn't sure. The instant friendship, the dinner invitations, evenings spent at the gallery … it would explain a lot.

What to do? I suspected that Galena and I were history. I'd decided long ago that Andrew was my chosen successor at Lanark Lighting. Could he be my successor in other ways, too? If so, it would solve a number of problems. But I would have to sort out the ramifications.

How to make Andrew realise that he and Galena were free to go their own way, with my blessing?

I would have to tell him so in plain text.

'Andrew – do you have a moment?'

He came back in.

'Andrew, this is very tricky, so I won't mince my words. Are you and Galena having an affair?'

Andrew's face was a picture. Shock. Was that fear? His mouth fell open. He went red, then white. He was speechless.

I raised a calming hand.

'Now don't worry', I said. 'I'm a man of the world. I know these things happen. Cupid's darts, and all that. There is a tide

Andrew. I Make a Mistake

in the affairs of men…who knows what the gods have in store for us…?'

I thought I might have been laying it on a bit thick. Andrew just gaped at me in horror.

'The point I want to make, Andrew – as a man of the world – is that, if you and Galena want to 'hook up' as they say … well, I'm the last person on earth to stand in your way. What I say is: go for it! And good luck to you both!'

I sat back, happy with my performance. I genuinely felt I was, at that moment, a highly civilised human being. The free-thinking legacy of the 60s, tempered by later, wiser counsels. A man of my times. Generous. Willing to step aside in the face of passion, magnetism, love … ready to suppress my own frayed feelings in the face of The Real Thing.

Andrew just stared at me. Then he slumped in his chair and his head fell forwards. At last he looked up at me.

'Guv … there's something I've been meaning to tell you.'

'Yes, Andrew. I expect there is.'

'The thing is, guv … I'm … actually … gay.'

Fuck.

'Andrew … I'm so sorry … I am *so* sorry … what can I possibly say?'

'I *was* going to tell you, but I wasn't sure what you'd think.'

What did I think?

Nothing. I liked Andrew more the better I knew him. So much so that I'd been about to pair him off with Galena, for all the world as if she were my daughter and he'd come to ask for her hand in marriage.

I felt like a complete idiot.

'I'm very sorry, Andrew. I feel like a complete idiot.'

I only knew one way to express an apology. Out came the Auchentoshan. Two big glasses.

Andrew. I Make a Mistake

'It's an easy mistake to make', said Andrew. 'Not your fault at all. But I'm glad you did – this is really good stuff.'

'I've offended you. Unforgiveable.'

'I'm not offended!' he said. 'I'm flattered, if anything. I like Galena and she's a stunner – anyone can see that. If I were that way inclined, I'd have bitten your arm off!'

He was doing his best to put me at my ease.

'Of course, I can tell that she might possibly be a bit of a handful.'

I glanced at him. Was it so obvious? But his face gave nothing away. Instead, he quoted from my national poet.

'Never met – or never parted, we had ne'r been broken-hearted'.

We raised our glasses to each other and thought quietly about handfuls we had known.

A Day at the Races

'Stirrups!'

Katerina Sokol had just asked me to name the innovation which transformed cavalry's effectiveness in the Dark Ages.

I had no idea, so I guessed: 'Chariots?'

A peal of laughter.

'No, you silly thing! They had chariots *thousands* of years ago.'

She seemed pleased to catch me out. 'Stirrups were brought to Europe by horsemen from the Steppes. They made all the difference. With stirrups the full force of horse and rider could be transmitted through a lance. Lethal!'

So now I knew.

I'd kept my word and taken Katerina on a tour of Barrandov Studios. Nothing much was happening but she was as excited as an eight-year-old on her birthday. It was obviously hallowed ground.

Now she was returning the favour. One of her father's horses was running at Prague's racecourse and I was her guest.

She picked me up in her yellow Carrera 4S. I wasn't surprised to see that she was an expert driver, weaving through the traffic like a marlin. We were there in less than thirty minutes.

There were eight races today. Sokol's horse, 'Foxbat', was entered for the last on the card – the 2,000 Guineas. In a field of sixteen Foxbat was an outsider, with not much form either good or bad.

Katerina pulled up in the Owners' Car-Park and leaped out. 'Come on!'

I was expecting a drink, but my host had other priorities. She grabbed my arm and pulled me along a path, through a

A Day at the Races

gate and across a patch of grass. It was an effort to keep up. She had longer legs than me.

We entered a gallery with horses' heads poking out of loose-boxes right and left, stretching away into the distance. I had a question to ask.

'Katerina, will you be riding Foxbat today?'

She turned to see if I was joking. When she saw that I was serious she doubled up with laughter.

'No, you silly thing, of course not! I do *eventing*! I could never ride a race-horse in a million years!'

'Why not?'

'Well, for one thing, I'm much too heavy. Jockeys are very special people – small, hard as screws and super-aggressive. They're almost a different species.'

'But I thought a good rider could do anything?'

'Well – it's not really true. Oh, I've ridden a few point-to-points in England – really good fun – but this is *serious racing*. It's professional. There's so much at stake.'

'2,000 Guineas? Your father must spend that on a decent lunch!'

'It's not the prize-money. It's the glory. The achievement. Most owners are rich people. That's why they call it the Sport of Queens.'

I was not going to correct Katerina's quaint version of English. In any case, I was no longer 'Mr Mackerel' but 'Ian' or, whenever I stepped out of my comfort zone, 'You silly thing'.

We were getting on like a house on fire. I had an uneasy conscience about this, not least because my real purpose in getting to know her was to bring her father's career, and life, to a violent end. But I couldn't help liking her. I told myself that my feelings were paternal. No, not that. Avuncular. Yes, avuncular.

A Day at the Races

She dragged me along to a box where a large, disdainful head scrutinized all the passing human beings and found them beneath contempt. Katerina stroked its nose and blew into its nostrils.

'Hello, Foxy. How are you today? Are you going to make Mummy and Daddy proud? Yes, you *are*. Of course you are!'

'Foxy' seemed to like this. His ears went forward and he lowered his head for more petting, which he got.

I moved a step nearer and the ears went back. One eye fixed me with a malevolent stare.

How did they know? It couldn't be smell. I'd drenched myself in 'Fahrenheit', knowing I'd be sitting next to Katerina in a small car. What then? It must be a sixth sense. I didn't like horses and they knew it, so they didn't like me. Or was it the other way round?

It turned out that jockeys didn't like me either. We were joined by a small person that I took to be a schoolboy. But it had the face of a gargoyle.

'Jiri! Ahoj! Jak se mas?'

Jiri got a kiss on both cheeks. Then they chattered away in Czech which obliged me, as usual, to kick my heels, feeling goofy and trying to look as if I were thinking about important things. I was really trying to catch an odd word I recognized. When Czechs spoke to each other I knew what it was like to be a dog. I could recognize my name and words like 'sandwich' but there was no possibility of comprehension.

Two more kisses and what was probably 'Good Luck!' from Katerina, then Jiri swaggered off, giving me a glance of pure loathing, just like the horse he would be riding in forty minutes' time.

'Isn't he sweet?'

'Yes, Katerina – very much so' I lied.

A Day at the Races

Now, at last, we made our way towards the drink I'd been gasping for. A special suite for owners and other VIPs. Deep carpets, leather armchairs. White-coated servants bringing drinks and canapes to groups of people who knew they were richer, special, different, superior. They all shared a look. Complacency? I tried it and failed.

Katerina didn't have the look, perhaps because she was too young. Or perhaps because she wasn't shallow.

A man of my own age approached us. He was a bit shorter than me and a lot shorter than Katerina, but his manner was hauteur incarnate. I went through a point-by-point check-list. Hair: his was an artificial black but expertly cut, mine was thicker. Face: his was tanned, mine was the mottled pink which identifies Scotsmen from Calgary to Kalgoorlie. Features: his were nothing special, mine, nothing special. Clothes: his dark-grey suit fitted him to perfection. There would be no label except, perhaps, a discreet patch on the inside of an inside pocket. Mine: it was my best suit. Boss. Off the peg.

I stopped there because I had lost. Or had I? Katerina greeted him in Czech, then said: 'May I introduce my new friend, Ian? He's an up-and-coming film producer.' At which she linked her arm through mine.

Mr Hauteur didn't miss a beat. 'Very pleased to make your acquaintance' he said, without a trace of an accent. The smile was artificial but fairly realistic.

'Do you have something running today?'

'Oh, no. I'm here to look and learn, courtesy of the Sokols.'

'Foxbat. Now there's a dark horse!'.

'Not really. He's a bay.' Katerina pretended to take him at his word.

'No, no, my dear – I simply meant that none of us know much about him. It's a metaphor.' *Smartarse.*

A Day at the Races

'Well, there's a good reason for that. He's spent most of his life in Virginia. Daddy and I bought him on sight when we were over there as guests of Mr and Mrs Arnold Bruckenheimer III'.

This was meant to shut him up and it worked. With a slight bow he moved off to inflict his charm on someone else.

'I'm sorry, Ian, but I really don't like him. I didn't mean to be rude.'

'Yes, you did, and I take my hat off to you.'

Katerina seemed pleased by the compliment.

'I didn't like him either,' I said. 'One look was all it took.'

'How do you do that? she asked.

'The same way Foxbat does, I suppose.'

'Foxy? But what do you mean? He's the *cutest* horse. Why, I've put my ten-year-old niece on his back and he was as good as gumdrops!'

I didn't want to admit that horses hated me on sight. At least, not to Katerina. I changed the subject.

'Now... I need to place my bet. How does one do that in these exalted surroundings?'

'It's easy. Just tell one of the waiters what you want and they'll run down to the window and do it for you. Unless, of course, you want to see what the bookmarkers are offering?'

I didn't. I'd seen the bookies' Bentleys lined up at every race-course I'd ever visited. I felt happier taking my chances with the pari-mutuel.

'It's Foxbat, of course' I said. 'But on the nose or place?'

I realised I was asking for insider information, but wasn't that the whole idea?

Katerina gave me a sidelong look.

'Well...' she said. 'I've always made a point of going for a place unless I have good reason to think that a particular horse

A Day at the Races

will sweep the table. There are some very fine horses in the 2,000 Guineas, and some very good jockeys too …'

A nudge is as good as a wink. I wanted to impress Katerina, so I beckoned to one of the waiters and produced a sheaf of 2,000 CZK notes from my back pocket. I counted out ten.

'Would you be so kind … Foxbat, each way.'

He scurried off. I was rewarded with a big smile from Katerina.

'And you …?' I enquired.

'Already done. My father has an arrangement.'

I should have known.

The time came. We went down to the paddock. Katerina blew kisses to Foxbat and Jiri. I made a kind of manly half-salute as they stalked past.

We went back up and out onto the VIP terrace. Starter's orders. I didn't need field-glasses. The course was small and from our vantage-point we could see everything that happened.

What happened was that Foxbat took the lead in the first furlong and held it all the way to the finish. He was three lengths ahead.

Katerina threw her arms round me and kissed me on both cheeks. Not the normal Czech greeting, but thought I could get used to it.

She had obviously known that Foxbat was a banker. But her sense of propriety didn't let her tell me so.

No complaints. I trousered a nice bundle of notes for my each-way bet.

We went back down for the parade. Katerina held Foxbat's halter, glowing. I was back where I belonged, a face in the crowd. I reminded myself that this brief glimpse into the lives of the super-rich was just that and no more.

A Day at the Races

Katerina was young, single-minded and evidently innocent. My proletarian principles meant nothing to her, and why would they? It was not her fault that she'd been brought up in the lap of luxury. In fact, I told myself in true Calvinist fashion, she deserved credit for reaching the age of nineteen without acquiring any airs and graces. We seemed to see life in much the same way.

But who was I kidding? Her world and mine were light-years apart. We could no more be real friends than fly to the moon. I wanted to protect her – *avuncular* - but couldn't. I was about to do the exact opposite.

I realised that I ought to be a lot less sentimental if I was going to have a future in the Department. 'Hard as screws'. The chance to test this stern resolve came sooner than I expected.

I re-joined Katerina and her team as they were putting Foxbat into his horse-transporter. It was a giant Scania with three axles and room for four horses in padded compartments. Foxbat didn't really want to enter, but a lot of cooing from Katerina and a bit of shoving from the grooms got him in and ready for his journey.

Where, I wondered.

'Where's he off to now, Katerina?'

'Warsaw. The Derby. It's the big one in Poland. It'll be tougher than this, poor thing. And the odds will be tighter. Why – are you thinking of backing him again?' Cheeky smile.

'I might. I believe in loyalty. After all, I'm a Hearts supporter.'

She looked baffled.

'It's a long, complicated story. I don't want to bore you. The bottom line is: my club/team/horse, win or lose.'

She looked baffled again.

A Day at the Races

'I'm confused. Isn't the idea to win?'

'Well ... yes and no. It's tricky. Some of us get a buzz from losing for years in the hope that one day – *one day* – we'll lift the trophy.'

She looked puzzled. I realised it would take a lifetime to describe the masochistic pleasure of backing Hearts or Hibs. Or Fulham. There was nothing like it in Katerina's world, and never had been.

In the car I considered what I had seen. A very large HGV which regularly travelled throughout Europe and beyond to move race-horses from one event to another. Accompanied, as often as not, by a golden-haired, nineteen-year-old woman, the daughter of the owner, the very picture of innocence – and a well-known equestrienne in her own right.

What better way could there be to ship arms from place to place, unsuspected and undetected?

I decided to share my suspicions with Fabian, wincing at the harm I might cause to my charming companion. But I was firm in my purpose: I had a *higher cause*.

'Hello, Forkbeard. This is Bloodaxe. Do we have a good line?'

'Yes, *Ian*. You know we do, or – I should say – you have every reason to expect that this connection is scrambled and impenetrable – though I might just add, if I may, that I appreciate your concern with security, as I am sure all my colleagues here in the Department do too ... anyway, what might it be, could I ask, that you wanted to impart? Hmm?'

Thirty words when ten would do. This was positive proof that I was speaking to Fabian. No AGI system could imitate him, and – even if it could – it wouldn't.

A Day at the Races

'Fabian, have you guys ever wondered how Sokol delivers his weapons without ever being apprehended at border controls?'

'Well... now you come to mention it, I would have to say ... yes, it has crossed our minds once or twice, but with no *particular* outcome to our speculations ... it remains, I have to admit, one of the many mysteries which surround the business activities of the gentleman you mention ... the how, when and where, so to say ... a branch of our studies which is, perhaps, most properly called logistics. Hmm?'

I gritted my teeth. This was Fabian at his most obtuse.

'OK, Fabian. I think I understand. You haven't the faintest idea how Sokol ships his cargoes around Europe? Or beyond?
'

'Hmm. Well, that would be a rather *harsh* way to describe the issue ... but I would have to agree that this particular aspect of the gentleman's commercial undertakings continues to present what one might describe as a dilemma to the Department's researchers and analysts. But never fear, Ian – we are famous (or, wearing another cap, notorious ha ha ha) for fathoming out the most knotty problems of this nature, given time. Or am I mixing my metaphors? That would never do ...'

I held my breath and counted to ten. Could it possibly be true that people like Fabian, responsible for the critical elements of UK national security, worried more about *mixing metaphors* than actually doing anything useful?

Yes, it could. I exhaled and continued.

'Horse-boxes.'

'I'm awfully sorry, Ian, I don't think I understand. Or perhaps I mis-heard. I thought you said *horse-boxes.*'

'I did. Horse-boxes. They travel from country to country full of animals. No-one inspects them apart from checking the

A Day at the Races

horses' passports. They are very large vehicles with lots of spaces and compartments. Sokol has three and other people like him have even more.'

There was a long silence.

'Ah. I think I am catching your drift, Ian. You are suggesting that people engaged in illicit commerce might be using horse-boxes as a way of evading the customs controls which are … shall we say … customary?'

He covered the phone to conceal the outburst of sniggering which followed this Shakespearean pun.

'Fabian … are you there?'

'Yes, Ian. Very much so. Food for thought, food for thought. May I ask … what led you to this rather intriguing insight? If I may enquire, without intruding? I had never thought of you as, so to speak, a 'racing man'. There's nothing to that effect on your file … are there hidden depths, Mr McKerrell? Should we begin to think of you as a member of the 'Cavalcade of The Turf'? Are you what one might call, in the vernacular, a bit of a 'railbird'? And, if so, and perhaps more to the point, could you provide a reliable tip for the 4.40 at Lingfield?'

Another burst of badly-concealed chuckling. I left him to it and rang off.

Good Dog

I put my head round the door. 'Mr McCoig, could I have a word?'

Sullenly, he got up and followed me along the corridor to my room.

'Please take a seat.'

Beaujolais growled. This never happened with anyone else, so I knew the dog agreed with me: there was something deeply unpleasant about McCoig.

I decided to keep the tone light.

'So how are you enjoying Prague?'

McCoig was slumped in the visitor's chair. He said nothing in reply and avoided my eyes. I tried again.

'Is this your first visit to the Czech Republic?'

Again, no response. Fair enough – if that's how he wanted to play it.

'I've got a bone to pick with you, McCoig.'

Beaujolais' ears pricked up. He didn't know about metaphors yet.

'Your personal behaviour is no concern of mine. I couldn't care less what you do or who you do it with. But what *is* my concern is the security of this operation. Shagging in the women's toilets is just about the best way I can think of to blow your cover and get tongues wagging.'

McCoig grunted. Beaujolais growled.

'What's more, it's not *your* safety that I'm bothered about. With any luck I'll never see either of you again. What *does* bother me is the risk you've carelessly inflicted on this company as a facility of Prague station.'

McCoig was staring at the wall and said nothing.

'Am I getting through to you, McCoig?'

Good Dog

He mumbled: 'Hackworth didn't mind'.

'Bugger Hackworth! He's here today and gone tomorrow, same as you. I live here and this company has been a Departmental asset for ten years. *That's* what you're stupidly putting in jeopardy.'

McCoig shifted in his chair. He looked up at last and leered.

'Did I jump the queue? Is that your problem?'

It took me a few moments to realise what the moron was implying.

I exploded. 'For fuck's sake, McCoig, no. That is *not* my problem. My problem is exactly what I've just tried to explain to you. *Security,* you idiot!'

McCoig returned to staring at the wall.

'Let me spell it out for you. This thing with Svetlana stops right now, and so do your other extra-mural activities, or I lodge a formal complaint with Fabian. Understand?'

No reply. McCoig got to his feet and shambled towards the door.

At that moment Beaujolais could resist no longer. With a high-pitched yip he leaped forward and sank his teeth into McCoig's ankle.

'Beaujolais! Leave!'

McCoig was squeaking. Beaujolais was growling. I was shouting. The door opened and Svetlana came in. She crouched down to the angry dog, whispered something, stroked his head and prised his jaws from McCoig's leg.

McCoig ran for it. Svetlana calmed Beaujolais, who had quickly decided that Svetlana was the best thing since Winalot. Then she made a joke.

'Your dog has no taste!'

Good Dog

I thought this was a bit rich in view of the topic of my conversation with the Glaswegian. 'But - what about – what about - you and him in the ladies' loo?'

Svetlana gave me a withering look as she left the room. I wouldn't understand what it meant for another week.

Beaujolais put his nose up for praise, tail wagging. He deserved it.

'Good dog!'

On the Road

The day came and the professionals shut down their laptops, tidied their papers and went back to their hotel. I went home to get ready. What to wear? I hadn't been trained for this. But I'd read the books and seen the films. I went for black jeans, a black shirt and a black ski-jacket. Did I need face camouflage? I put a tin of boot-polish in my pocket, just in case.

At 2am – or 0200 hours as Hackworth put it – I rolled up in my Volvo to collect them. Yes. Dull. But I was trying to project the image of a sensible, grown-up family man. That's what our clients wanted. They weren't to know that I wasn't grown up and didn't have a family. But the car said it for me.

Hackworth was already suited and booted in neoprene. I was tempted to make a fetish joke, but didn't. This was serious. He covered up with jeans and a jacket. McCoig wore Wranglers, a mauve T-shirt and a brown anorak. His charm, brains and dress-sense were all of a piece.

We set off for Tabor, a two-hour drive at slow speed. We wound our way through the city and joined Route 3 at Nusle. I was taking it easy ... 100 kph. I didn't want to attract the attention of the Dopravni policie. But I was out of luck.

We were chuntering along the motorway when I saw flashing lights in my mirror. 'Damn!' 'Don't worry', said the rubber-clad Hackworth. Why not? Of course I was worried. I pulled over.

A female police officer got out of the car and came up to my window. Like so many of her kind, she could have been a cover-model. She said something incomprehensible in Czech. I said: 'Anglicky – nemluvim cesky, prominte'. She smiled: 'May I see your driver's licence please?' I got it out of my pocket and handed it to her.

On the Road

Meanwhile Hackworth had slid out of the car and gone round to stand next to her, helpfully. There was a thud and she slid to the ground with a groan.

'Give me a hand' said Hackworth. We dragged her into the bushes beside the road. 'What about the car?' I gibbered. Hackworth got in, doused the lights and drove the Octavia into the trees.

'Let's go' he said. 'But ... but ... ' I wanted to say something but I didn't know what to say.

'Calm down, Ian. You have to expect a bit of collateral. It's normal'.

A young woman had been violently assaulted. It meant nothing to Hackworth.

'By the time she comes round we'll be safely back in Prague.'

We were approaching Tabor. This was where it would get difficult.

But Hackworth wanted to chat. 'Interesting what they teach you at Hambleside' he confided. 'The great thing is to get the job done without any unnecessary mess – you know, blood and so on. The fewer traces the better, if you see what I mean. These forensic chaps can be a bit of a nuisance these days. That's why I very rarely use a handgun. Hardly ever. Too many contaminants, and we don't want that'

He waggled his fingers.

To my horror, Hackworth seemed to be looking forward to his encounter with Sokol. I edged away as far as I could.

'Of course, sometimes it's unavoidable' he mused. 'But even then, they teach you to minimize the fluids – knife into the kidneys, diagonal stab into the jugular ... the great thing is to keep the blade in until the heart stops beating. You see the point, don't you?'

On the Road

I did. But he wouldn't stop.

'Ideally, one wants to extinguish life without leaving any evidence. But that's a tough call … what Hambleside calls A-plus. Get a couple of those under your belt and you're well on your way, I can tell you.'

It was like listening to a Stephen King character but in real life. Was this the same man who'd trembled with excitement at seeing Leonardo DiCaprio on a film-set? Yes, it was.

I couldn't help myself, sitting next to this weirdo. 'What was the hardest job you've ever had to do – I believe you call it termination with extreme prejudice?'

Hackworth chuckled. 'You've been watching too many films! No, we call it 'retiring'. We 'retire' people who are putting Western civilization at risk. Chummy tonight is a good example. He's blown smoke into everyone's eyes by funding Czech training camps, but all the while he's making his money by selling MANPADS and Javelins to Hezbollah. Which means Iran. And Assad.'

'Oh'.

He didn't answer my question but saw the opportunity for a lecture.

'Someone's got to shut down these madmen. No-one in Europe wants anything to do with it. But we do. We have a tradition of – what can I call it – *realism*. It goes back a long way, long before SOE and long before the derring-do of the First World War. Might even go back to Tudor times …'

On and on. Why and how Hackworth and his colleagues were noble enough to stand in the front line against our surreptitious enemies. How and why their bravery was all we had to protect ourselves from extinction. On and on.

I had to interrupt the sermon.

'But isn't there a better way – isn't that what diplomacy is all about? Can't we resolve our differences without breaking people's necks?'

Hackworth chuckled again. It meant 'How little you know!' Then he spoke.

'It all depends whose rules you're playing by. You're right – in an ideal world there would be no need for conflict, at any level. Sensible people would talk to other sensible people and they'd reach a compromise. A bit like the Oxford Union Society. Are you an Oxbridge man?'

I knew he knew I wasn't. I also knew that no-one called it 'Society'.

'No. You?'

'Could have been, so I'm told. But life intervened, you might say.'

'So your point is … that people are not really civilized? Is that it?'

'Yes. We make all the right noises, and we have the UN, the WTO and a thousand other do-gooding organisations telling us how things ought to be. In the end, they don't make a blind bit of difference. When push comes to shove, it's all about brute force.'

'That sounds bleak, to say the least. Are you discounting all the thinking and progress we've made since Athens?'

I was on shaky ground. I didn't know very much about democracy.

Hackworth did.

'Don't make me laugh! Athens was a *slave-state*. The only reason some of them could turn up on the *pnyx* to vote was that they had an army of captives labouring away to an early death in the mines. The idea that Athens was the cradle of civilization is a bad joke.'

On the Road

I didn't know enough to argue. But Hackworth didn't want a conversation.

'Look what happened as soon as Athens felt threatened or fancied a bit of territorial expansion! They couldn't wait to get their spears and shields off the wall and rush out onto the battlefield. Why do think they loved Homer so much?'

I had no answer.

'Because the Iliad is a glorification of blood and guts from start to finish, that's why! Homer is the Hellenic version of Ernst Jünger.'

Hackworth and Cassandra could have had an interesting discussion. But she'd probably run a mile. At least, I hoped so.

He'd lost me and he knew it. All he was trying to do was prove his point. He succeeded. He carried on talking but I stopped listening. I felt certain he was wrong, but I couldn't say why.

Time passed. I drove on at a steady 100 kph.

'So there you have it! Everything significant in recorded history has been won or lost at the point of a sword. It's no different today. You can forget about nuclear weapons.'

Could I? The spectre of nuclear war had loomed over my life from the day I was born. We were trained to get under the tables in our classroom as five-year-olds. How could anyone forget that?

'You have to understand that the principle of mutually-assured destruction *really works*. What actually matters is done *man-to-man*, as it always has been and always will be. Did you know the Germans killed 1.7 times as many of their enemies as we did – per man, in person?'

I was tempted to ask why, in that case, they lost. But I didn't want to encourage him. I'd heard enough.

On the Road

I was beginning to understand Hackworth's mentality. To his way of thinking, nothing had changed. Civilised nations still depended on bloodthirsty maniacs like him to keep the peace. He saw himself as Achilles. Horatius on the bridge. Leonidas. He didn't see himself as a psycho. He saw himself as a hero.

Perhaps a professional assassin needed to take refuge in some kind of fantasy mental world. I didn't know and I didn't care. All I knew was that I wanted to get this 'operation' over as soon as possible and then never speak to Hackworth, or anyone like him, ever again.

Tabor

At last we reached the outskirts of Tabor. I was feeling nervous, but in a strange way Hackworth's psychopathic tendencies reassured me. He had come to seem like someone I could rely on in these peculiar circumstances.

I glanced in the mirror. McCoig was gazing at the trees beside the road. Was he thinking of the mission, or Svetlana, or three young women at Le Chiffre? Or anything at all? Most people give you some indication of what they're like, but McCoig was an exception. I decided to forget about him. If Hackworth thought McCoig was an efficient killer, that was good enough for me. I was, after all, just the driver.

Tabor. A good choice for someone who wanted isolation. It was miles from anywhere in the middle of a gently rolling landscape laid down millions of years ago when Central Europe was at the bottom of the sea. Other parts of the Czech Republic had extinct volcanoes, river-valleys and dramatic rock formations, but not here. Just lakes, forests and undulating farmland.

Its isolation made it attractive to the military. You could still see the remains of huge sheds where the Germans hid their Panzer fleets. Perhaps this was homage to the Hussites, Europe's original tank-army. Here and there you could still spot the gaunt outlines of Intermediate-Range Missile Sites left over from the Soviet era, now crumbling into concrete dust and twisted iron. But most of it was featureless. The town and its local lakes were popular with hikers and school-parties, but the region was not on many tourist maps.

Sparsely inhabited and agricultural, Tabor gave Sokol the privacy he needed and, so it seemed, the private lake his daily fitness routine required.

Tabor

We had come to the turn-off for Sokol's estate, but Hackworth chatted away as if we were sitting in a pub. 'The way I see it' he continued, 'is that it's us or them. Same story since time began'. Was he quoting Hegel or Nietzsche? I knew nothing much about either, so I didn't have a lot to contribute to the conversation. But it had never been a conversation.

'Get in there first – that's my motto. Failing that, for every one they give you, give them back three!' I glanced across. He was leaning back in his seat, apparently relaxed and comfortable. He was due to murder a stranger with his bare hands before sunrise.

He couldn't stop talking. 'The thing is' … . I groaned inwardly. 'The thing is that *they* make their own rules and don't expect *us* to follow them. They'll cheerfully stick poisoned pellets into dissidents and give Polonium tea to someone they think is out of order. But they think *we* flinch when it comes to doing the same thing back at them. Well – McCoig and me are here to show them different. I call it a level playing-field.'

I glanced across again. His expression could only be described as contented. I wondered if his grammar was a symptom of pre-action adrenaline.

'So it's us or them? No entente, no détente?'

I got no answer. Hackworth simply wanted me to know that there was a firm moral basis for his barbaric role in life. It occurred to me that he'd given this lecture many times before, usually to lesser mortals just like me, in Estonia, Venezuela, Nigeria, Serbia…

Did he have a point? Lots of Americans once thought it was wrong for the United States to possess nuclear weapons when the Soviet Union didn't. They created their own 'level playing-field', from whatever motives, and some of them ended up in the electric chair. Or in a Christopher Nolan movie.

Hackworth, in his peculiar way, was a moralist. But I'd heard enough. He was knowledgeable and his enthusiasm for things like The Movies could be endearing, but I didn't warm to him. Like most people, I was inclined to accept ideas if they came from someone I admired. If they were said by someone I despised, they fell on stony ground, regardless of merit. I knew this was a primitive way to form my opinions, but I also knew I wasn't a deep thinker. That was what Father Dominic was for.

The surface was bumpier and I slowed down. This must be a pre-independence road, a remnant of Warsaw Pact Czechoslovakia. Potholed, falling apart, barely maintained, if at all. But just right for Sokol's privacy.

We reached the edge of the lake. It was pitch dark and I couldn't see a thing. But Hackworth could. He was in his element. I nudged forward, then turned carefully and edged the Volvo into a grove of willows.

I shut down the engine and everything was quiet. There was a slight breeze, but not enough to disturb the placid waters of Sokol's private reservoir. I got out of the car and tried to get my bearings. Though the landscape here was flat, I was reminded of the lochs of southern Scotland. Broad, self-contained acres of fresh water, dark and often surprisingly deep. There was something sinister about it. Did it contain monsters? On this particular morning, I thought, there'd be at least two.

The banks sloped gently, thick with reeds and bullrushes. A haven for wildlife. I could hear the first geese and ducks waking up. What were they? I had no idea, but there were ten species of goose and thirty kinds of duck in this part of the country. I could also hear owls, telling us off for disturbing

Tabor

their hunting. As dawn approached, other, invisible things began croaking and whirring.

The Czechs were obsessed with nature and the countryside. They loved it with a passion. I admired them for it. But for me, the open landscape meant midges and twisted ankles. It wasn't my thing. I was a townie.

But here I was.

Hackworth had opened the boot and was quietly taking off his jeans and jacket. There was no sign of a gun, knife or harpoon. I asked him why not. He waggled his fingers at me yet again. 'No need! If you've done Hambleside you don't need *accoutrements*. They just complicate things and risk leaving traces. We're not *Russians*, you know.'

I guessed he was referring to the Salisbury poisonings, which I and many others thought so incompetently handled that it must have been deliberate. As if the Russians were saying: 'We can do what we like in your country, and we don't even need to create a convincing cover-story. Here are some idiots to talk to your TV stations!' It had been this affront, over and above the attempted homicides, which made my blood boil, and I was one of many. A lot of people concluded that the Russians had finally lost the plot.

'OK. I'm sure you know best. Now – what do you want me and McCoig to do while you're … doing whatever you're going to do?'

'Good point. Glad you asked. Perhaps *you* could remain near the car. We may need to make a quick getaway - though I doubt it. Keep a sharp look-out for extraneous bodies. But there shouldn't be any.'

'And what should I do if I spot an *extraneous body*?'

Tabor

'Umm.. good question. If I were you I'd make myself scarce … get under the car, or something. Then let us know. Can you hoot?'

What?

'Can you make a noise like an angry owl?'

'I don't know. '

'Well, have a go.'

I felt ridiculous but I obeyed his instructions. We'd all done this when I was nine years old. Cupping my hands in front of my mouth, I hooted.

'Perfect! You win this year's Star Prize for Owl Impersonation! Ta-da!'

'Shouldn't we be trying to keep quiet?' I hissed.

'Oh, yes. *Stay hush, chaps.*'

My role was obviously not meant to be heroic. I felt a sense of relief but also something like disappointment.

'McCoig' hissed Hackworth. 'Over here! Now – I want you to loiter with intent, if you see what I mean'.

McCoig's blank face showed no sign of emotion or even comprehension.

'Let me spell it out. While *I'm* in the water *you* are responsible for giving me cover on the bank. Got it?'

A faint smile animated McCoig's features for the first time. He produced a long-barrelled pistol with what looked like a Coke can attached to the muzzle. He raised an eyebrow.

'Fine' said Hackworth. 'Just make sure you see them before they see you.'

McCoig's eyebrow moved up to his hairline. This had to be Glaswegian for 'as if…'

I got the impression that McCoig was hoping to use his weapon before the night was out. This made me anxious. But

Tabor

if Hackworth, the sunny assassin, was confident, what did my opinion matter?

Hackworth glanced at his watch. 'Right. I'm going in. Our friend will set off for his two-kilometre constitutional at 0500 hours. I'll meet him about 100 metres out, do the necessary and tow him back to shore. He goes in the back of the Volvo and we'll dump him in a ditch where no-one will look for a hundred years. Clear?'

I nodded. I was a spear-carrier. I knew how Andrew felt. But at least I could do what was expected of me: watch, listen, hoot and roll under the car.

What about McCoig? He nodded too.

It all seemed very straightforward. Hackworth would play the starring role. McCoig and I would hover in the wings. Simple and clear-cut.

But it didn't turn out like that at all.

Cold Water

Hackworth slid into the lake and began swimming. I had to admit that he was good. Barely a ripple. He was soon out of sight, surging off towards the spot where Sokol would meet his fate.

I was left to think my own thoughts. What did I know of Sokol? Not much. I'd met him at Galena's vernissage but he'd left no impression apart from his obvious attachment to his daughter, Katerina. Like most relics of the Soviet system he gave nothing away. All the older Czechs I met were like that. In those days a careless word or even the wrong facial expression could mean the Gulag or death. They learnt to face the world behind a mask.

What else? He was one of those people, common in the aftermath of the Warsaw Pact, who'd risen without trace. He'd gone, almost overnight, from nothing to billionaire. Everyone 'knew' this was all about armaments and munitions, but the factual evidence was thin. He was a careful man.

He owned the estate in South Bohemia, properties in Montenegro and Slovenia, a house in Upper Grosvenor Street, and a 50-metre motor-yacht registered in Vanuatu. This much was on the public record. But what else did we know? Nothing substantive. I had to accept the Department's assertion that Sokol was selling arms to Iran-backed terrorists and other undesirables.

Sokol gave a lot of money to Czech equestrian teams and provided lavish support for hockey, football, skiing, athletics ... A shrewd PR strategy? But why did this faceless man need PR? Whatever the reason – maybe he just liked sports – it made him popular among the Czechs, who neither knew nor cared about the source of his wealth.

Cold Water

But this was irrelevant to the CIA and the SIS. What mattered to them was not how he spent his money but how he made it.

I couldn't reconcile the idea of Sokol's picture-book family with images of a thousand torn bodies in Manchester or two hundred holidaymakers blown to bits in Bali. I realised that I wanted Hackworth to succeed. Sokol was an instrument of mass-murder. He deserved to die.

'Get him, Hackworth!' I said to myself. 'Kill the bastard!'

I waited silently and motionless for something to happen. The minutes ticked by. I couldn't see McCoig. I couldn't see anything much.

There was a rustle in the bushes behind me. I turned round to see three or four dim shapes approaching the car. If I couldn't see *them* they probably couldn't see *me*. I decided to ignore Hackworth's advice and slithered down to the water's edge, beneath the bank. It was reedy and muddy. I felt sure I was invisible.

I sank down until only my eyes and nose were above water. It was freezing.

I heard voices whispering in Czech. What were they saying? I wished I'd spent more time in the language lab. Too late now.

What were they doing here? They could only be Sokol's guards. Our brief said they would be sound asleep in their barracks while Sokol enjoyed his early-morning swim. Note to self: never believe what you are told.

Where was McCoig and his silenced hand-gun? He must have spotted these intruders. Why wasn't he dealing with them? *Where was he?*

Too late now. They'd surrounded the car and there was nothing I could do. Except hoot. I raised my hands and blew air through my lips. It sounded like a dying moorhen. Useless.

Cold Water

My hands and face were too cold and wet. Not a problem I'd encountered at Lanark Primary. What could I do?

As it turned out, I didn't need to do anything. I heard four muted reports – pop-pop-pop-pop – and the four guards collapsed. I looked towards the source of the noise. In the dim light I thought I saw a figure I recognized. Not McCoig. Female. It looked very much like Svetlana.

Svetlana? What on earth would my PA, of all people, be doing here on the bank of Sokol's private lake, hidden in the trees? It must be an illusion. I was seeing things. But the evidence was right there before my eyes: four guards, efficiently disposed of with four silenced rounds. I thought the figure I spotted in the half-light resembled Svetlana, but that was obviously nonsense. It must have been McCoig. Though taller.

But where *was* McCoig, with his Beretta? He was nowhere to be seen. I couldn't make head nor tail of this. But then I had other things to worry about.

I was lurking, more or less submerged, underneath the bank. I couldn't see very much in the twilight but my ears were on high alert. I heard something that made my blood run cold.

Quiet, rhythmic splashing. Someone approaching me in the water. It couldn't be Hackworth – he was miles away. Who, then? It could only be one of Sokol's men. My blood froze.

The splashing came nearer. I tried to make myself as small as possible. I sank down until only my nose was above the water-line. I stopped breathing.

Then a massive blow on top of my head. Then nothing.

I came round some time later. I was propped on a log and Hackworth was sitting next to me. My eyes didn't work properly. I had a bad headache.

'All right, old son?' said a familiar, cheery voice. 'He nearly got you!'

Cold Water

'What... who... what do you mean? What happened?'

Hackworth examined my face. First-aid. He was frowning.

'You got clobbered by Sokol's fifth guard. As luck would have it, I wasn't far away, so I managed to stop things going any further.'

'What do you mean?'

Hackworth gestured towards the waters of the lake. I could dimly make out a large body floating a few feet from the bank, face-down.

'Him!' said Hackworth happily. 'He sneaked up and bashed you but he never thought to look behind his own back!'

Hackworth seemed offended by this lack of professionalism.

'Anyway, he won't be troubling us any more. He's learnt a useful lesson.'

I wasn't in the mood for Hackworth's graveyard humour. Nor for his relentless cheerfulness.

'Ready, Eddie? Hot to trot? Good to go? Shall we make tracks?'

I felt like death, but Hackworth's chatter was worse than death. I meekly said yes.

The Journey Home

Hackworth was driving in his wet-suit. I was in the passenger seat, navigating, teeth chattering. I was wearing his clothes. Mine were in a bin-liner in the back, next to two other bin-liners containing Sokol.

'Feeling a bit better, are we?'

'Ugh'.

'I know, I know … the trouble is' (I groaned inwardly) 'you have to expect a few knocks, now and then, when you're engaged in operational work'.

'But I'm not! I'm a *facility*! I do bank accounts and provide people like you with cover … that's all! I'm a respectable businessman!'

Hackworth took his eyes of the road for a second.

'And Svetlana? Is she part of your facility? What was *she* doing at Sokol's lake?'

So he'd spotted her. I'd been right.

'I really haven't the faintest idea. She's a secretary, for goodness' sake.'

What else could I say? I was as mystified as he was.

'What bothers me is how and why Sokol's security people were there, waiting for us. There must have been a leak.' Hackworth was troubled.

So was I.

'What bothers *me* is why McCoig did absolutely nothing to look after us. Wasn't he supposed to be our sentry? Where was he?'

'Yes. Good point. Odd. We'll have to find out.'

Hackworth didn't seem inclined to speculate about McCoig's performance. But I didn't want to let it go.

The Journey Home

'Or, to be fair, was it McCoig who dispatched the four guards and then, for unknown reasons, disappeared?'

Hackworth grunted. 'No. McCoig had a Beretta M9. Those shots came from a CZ 75. Unmistakeable. Whoever took care of the guards it wasn't McCoig. We need to know who it was, and *we will find out*. Trust me on that.'

We drove on. It was a clear night and the roads were fairly empty. My head was throbbing but I was curious.

'The actual operation ... how did that go? If I may ask?'

'You mean Sokol?'

'Yes.'

'Pretty straightforward, really. There he was, thrashing along. I swam up behind him and well ... you know'.

'I don't mean to pry – how exactly did you did it?'

Hackworth took his hands off the wheel for a moment and waggled his fingers.

We drove on. I didn't need to do much navigating. None, actually. Every couple of kilometres a big green sign said PRA-GUE. Just as well. My brain was running on two cylinders. But it was still more or less functioning.

'Adrian ... I need to say something. I *want* to say something'.

'Oh yes? what might that be?'

He overtook a truck at 160 kph.

'*Slow down, for Christ's sake! Remember you don't have a driving-licence!*'

'Is that it?'

'No, of course not. What I want to say is ... I'm very grateful. I don't know how to put it, but ... if it weren't for you I'd be eel-food by now. So thank you very much.'

Hackworth glanced at me with a grin. 'Think nothing of it! All in a day's work! All part of the service!'

The Journey Home

But I could tell he was pleased. He accelerated until the chassis of the Volvo was shaking almost as much as I was.

We reached Prague alive, somehow, and Hackworth dropped me off at my flat.

'I'll walk back to the hotel. You'll be right as rain in a day or so, but get a doctor to check for concussion. I don't suppose we'll meet again, but thanks a lot for your help. You did really well. Shame about McCoig. Not good. We'll find out what happened. Anyway, all the best!' He grinned and sauntered off towards the Hilton.

I staggered into my flat feeling sorry for myself. Beaujolais jumped up and licked my face. I didn't mind – it was the most human experience I'd had in two days. I looked around. There was no sign of Galena, or her clothes. Beaujolais needed feeding. There was no excuse for that.

Double Winalot. And a slab of svickova that I'd been saving for my next romantic dinner with Galena. Karma! Then I told myself to stop being pathetic and get on with it.

I put some Arnica ointment on my head and checked my watch. 9 am. I rang the office. Andrew answered. 'Hi, guv, I was just about to ring you. Those idiots in Luton sent the wrong grids. Too big. We can't use them. It's *tomorrow*. Do you think one of your mates could help us out?'

Back to normal. Thank goodness. I wouldn't hear from the Department for a long time, and I didn't want to.

Back to Work

I took a day off to recover. I made a fuss of Beaujolais, re-organised my books – title, author or subject? I could never decide – and cooked a couple of things for the freezer. I was bored stiff, so I decided my recovery was complete.

Czechs like to start work early and I'd caught the habit. I limped up the stairs at 8 am and fell into my chair. I felt as if I'd been away for weeks.

'Kava?' said a familiar voice. It was Svetlana. She was demurely dressed in a red skirt and white sweater. Hardly any make-up, sunny smile.

'You!' I managed to say. 'You ... here ...'

'Yes. Of course. It is eight o'clock'.

I didn't know what to think. Svetlana had been seen at Tabor and she definitely wasn't part of our team. That meant she was working for the other side. Or some other side. Yet here she was, bright and early, acting as if nothing had happened. Was I mad? Was I missing something? Or did Svetlana simply have cast-iron *cojones*?

I didn't have time to consider the biological probabilities before Svetlana opened her laptop and said: 'Shall we go through the diary?'

We went through the diary.

Whenever I glanced up she was sitting there quietly, the picture of the perfect administrator. She had a slight smile on her face, as she always did whenever she wasn't whooping and yelling with the other young women in the main office. She knew something ... something I didn't know. I looked at her more closely.

Svetlana wasn't my type – we both knew that, and there'd been no embarrassing moments at Christmas parties. I wasn't

Back to Work

her type either. She flirted all day long with anything wearing trousers – clients, suppliers, the Pizza Hut boy, the UPS man. She made a point of leaning over Andrew's shoulder very closely, glancing round to make sure that everyone else could see what she was doing. It was blatant.

I began to wonder again if this wasn't all a carefully-contrived act. Did Svetlana have a secret agenda? What *had* she been doing at Tabor? Was she an enemy or an ally? I was intrigued, to say the least. If it *was* her at Tabor, how had she managed to dispatch Sokol's guards with four clean shots? That certainly wasn't something you learnt at secretarial school.

And, now I thought about it, she had exceptionally fine legs. And the figure of an ice-skater.

I would have to stop this. But the mystery made Svetlana interesting, and that somehow made me see her in a new light. She was an unusual creature, no doubt about it. Clever. Efficient. Attractive.

But what was I thinking? She must be half my age! I quickly did the maths … 45 divided by two … twenty-two and a half. No, Svetlana must be at least 25, probably more. I felt an obscure sense of relief.

No, McKerrell, get a grip! She's way too young, she's an employee and for all you know she's working for the FSB! *Stop right now!*

But then… what did age really matter? Didn't every Czech oligarch have a girlfriend or wife younger than his own daughters? That wasn't an example I wanted to emulate. But then… what *did* I want? Galena was soon to be history – or I was. If it wasn't Andrew it would be someone else. Or maybe no-one … just not me. Did I plan on living alone?

No, I didn't. I wasn't twenty-five or even thirty-five. I was, shall we say, in the prime of life. I wanted a partner, a companion … perhaps a wife. It was time to start thinking about a family. I had Beaujolais, of course … but only a cynic would think of a dog as a substitute. Anyway, Labradors like children.

And here was a candidate. Bright, clever, full of life. Hidden depths.

When I looked up Svetlana was sitting there with her laptop, a faint smile on her face. She looked straight at me and seemed to know exactly what was going through my mind.

A Demonstration

I was curious. What exactly *were* martial arts, and what part did they play in the life of my PA outside the office?

I decided to find out.

It was 5pm and the Czechs had all grabbed their coats and run for the tram. They were phenomenal time-keepers … never a minute late to arrive, never a minute late to leave.

Svetlana, as usual, was putting things straight before heading off to whatever athletic pursuit she had scheduled for this evening.

'Lana …'

'Yes, Ian?'

'I've been meaning to ask … if you have a minute … only if you're not rushing away, that is … '

'Yes, of course. What is it?'

'Well, I was wondering … you know all this *martial arts* stuff you talk about on the Team section of the website …'

'Yes.'

'Well, what I wondered was – I ought to know, but I don't … *what is it?*'

'Ah. A simple enquiry. It deserves a simple answer. I expect you know about the principles of self-defence?'

'Yes, I think so. More or less.'

'And you know how important it is to keep oneself fit?'

I wasn't sure what to say. I was a good two kilos overweight.

'Yes, I *know* about it, though I'm not a very good illustration.'

'I've seen worse. Much worse. You're in fairly good shape for a man of – what are you? – forty?'

Forty? I was immediately flooded with serotonin, dopamine and endorphins. As Svetlana no doubt intended.

A Demonstration

'Spot-on!' I lied. 'You must have been looking at the personnel files.'

'Anyway, when you put together *self-defence* and *keeping fit* what you get is martial arts. Or in my personal case *krav maga*.'

It rang a vague bell. I thought it meant street-fighting.

'Would you like a small demonstration?'

Yes, I would.

'Now: you stand there,' instructed Svetlana, 'And I will be here.'

We took up our positions.

'Now: you must come at me as if you want to attack me, steal my handbag or even kill me!'

I moved hesitantly towards her.

'Not like that! You have to *mean* it! Put some energy into it! You are a deranged drug-addict or a psychopath who wants to do me harm! The whole point of *krav maga* is for me to turn your energy against you.'

I tried again, this time a bit quicker and with more intention.

Suddenly, I don't know how, I was face-down on the floor and Svetlana was about to break my arm. 'Ow! Stop it!'

She stopped it. I got up, disconcerted. 'How on earth did you do that?'

'Well, it's nothing special. Very basic *krav maga* technique.' She was entirely unruffled, while I was ruffled. 'I hope I didn't hurt you?'

'No, no, not at all. But how did you do it?'

'Shall we try again?'

'Yes ... love to ... but could it be – well – a bit slower?'

Svetlana smiled. We took up our positions. This time I threw myself at her. This time I found myself face-up on the floor with my PA on top of me. She smiled again. I could not move.

A Demonstration

'Is this what you wanted me to do?' she enquired.
I could not speak.
Slowly, Svetlana lowered her face to mine.
Some time later we locked up the office and walked hand-in-hand to The Lemon Leaf for Gaeng Keow Wan Gai.

The Review

A peremptory email. 'You are required to attend a meeting at 1400 hours on the 5th June at Vauxhall Cross, Room 717, in order to account for your activities in connection with the tragic demise of Mr Stepan Sokol in the neighbourhood of Tabor in the Czech Republic on or about the 15th May ... by order of ... etc etc.'

WHAT?

I was a facility, paid almost nothing and considered a mere functionary in the Department's scheme of things. Why should I, of all people, make my way to the South Bank – at my own expense – to take part in one of the Department's witch-hunts? Why me? What did I have to gain? Nothing. What did I have to lose? It was a long list.

But I had no choice.

The head of the Department, Sir Reginald Handiside, was, to all intents and purposes, God. He looked the part. Ageless, though obviously old. Domed head, not much hair, made up for by a bushy grey beard and a moustache which hid his mouth. Schoolmaster's specs, wrinkled forehead, permanent frown.

We all knew that he was the son of a war hero – a real one. Kenneth Handiside had been the sole survivor of our Netherlands network. Everyone else had been captured and executed by the Germans. They'd been betrayed, and how Handiside escaped was the stuff of Departmental legend.

But to the general public he was unknown, and his son was just another faceless civil servant. Sir Reginald liked it that way. He wasn't the type to write his memoirs, and the thought of appearing on TV would have given him a cardiac arrest.

'It has come to our attention ...'

The Review

I was sitting with all the other unimportant people on a chair against the wall. Everyone who mattered was seated round the table. I was intrigued to see that one of them was Hackworth.

'The question therefore arises … who or what could have been responsible for Mr Sokol's unfortunate demise and is there any possibility, however remote, that the Department could have been, or might find itself, implicated in this heinous act.'

Various people said various things. I did my best to concentrate but I'd travelled in on an early flight and I was short of sugar, caffeine, or maybe alcohol. I drifted.

Suddenly there was a command: 'Clear the room!' I got up and went out with everyone else. Then an usher came up and whispered in my ear: 'Please come back in'.

There were only seven people round the table. I was invited to join them.

Sir Reginald said: 'Right. Now that fol-de-rol's out of the way, let's get down to business'.

Someone interrupted: 'Excuse me, Sir – when you say 'fol-de-rol' do you actually mean 'crap'?'

He glowered. 'You know exactly what I mean. Don't try to be clever.'

Then he got to the point.

'This was an excellent operation which achieved its objective without the slightest possibility of culpability being assigned to this Department or HMG. We know this because those ninnies outside have done their best but have come up with, if I may use the phrase, bugger-all'.

He looked at each of us with what may have been a smile.

'I therefore wish to congratulate you all, individually and collectively, on very good work – a difficult task, well done.

The Review

Your reward, as you know, will be in heaven. We cannot publicly admit to… this kind of thing. But you know, and I know, and HMG knows, and our American allies know, that you have made the world a safer place for free people living in democracies'.

I was stunned. So *this* was how it really worked?

Sir Reginald expanded on his theme.

'It's regrettable, I think we'd all agree, but it's reality. The organs of government – the FCO and so on.' he paused while everyone smiled…'the official representatives of HMG do what they can to minimize the apparent risks to us and our allies. But their hands are tied.'

He looked round at each of us.

'Our opponents, let us call them, enjoy the luxury of untied hands. Be they rogue governments or small-scale malefactors, they can and do resort to extreme physical solutions which are outside the *apparent* capabilities of the democratic polities. You don't need a list … Markov, Manchester Arena, Salisbury …'

Everyone nodded gravely.

'And that's where we come in, Ladies and Gentlemen. I like to think of it as shortening the odds. Once these Charlies see that we can and will strike back – below the level of visibility, so to speak, and below the belt – they begin to realise that their hands are tied after all.'

He stopped speaking and leant back in his chair. He surveyed us all benignly, and must have pressed a hidden button.

Waiters entered and distributed glasses of Glenmorangie 19-Year-Old.

'Here's tae us, an' wha's like us?' said Sir Reginald.

'Gey few, an' they're aw deid!' we roared.

An Invitation

Hackworth and I left together. 'Do you fancy a pint? I know a great place for Landlord just near here.'

'I suppose you know what that was all about' he said after his first swig.

'Not really.'

'Well, old chap, it's the gap between what *has* to be done and what can be admitted in public. We talked about this in the car, if you remember?'

Did I? I knew he'd bent my ear for nearly two hours but most of it had gone in one and out of the other.

'Can I say something?'

Could I stop him?

'What I wanted to say is that … well … I was really quite impressed by the way you took on the job of driving us down to Tabor … you had no warning, and of course the Department and I apologise for that … but, you know, needs must and so on … what I really wanted to say – well, I don't know how you'll take this …'

He took another gulp of Landlord.

'Well, to come to the point and to make no bones about it … there are various people who think you could have a future in what we might call the *operational* side of the Department's activities.'

I stared at him.

'Only if it appeals to you, of course. It's certainly not everyone's cup of tea… you know, some people have what you might call moral problems with this kind of work, and some people are just a bit too squeamish …'

I thought back to the blithe way Hackworth had disposed of the Czech policewoman. Nothing squeamish about him. In

An Invitation

Hackworth's vocabulary, 'innocent bystander' just meant 'collateral damage'. If he considered it at all.

I didn't know what to say, so I went to the bar for two more pints. The last time I'd been involved in physical combat was playing rugby for Lanark's youth team. I didn't expect to meet that level of deliberate violence again until the day I died.

'I'm just not sure' I told Hackworth. 'Would I really be cut out for it? I want to do everything I can for the Department, obviously, and I must say I'm very flattered by what you say, but … I don't know.'

'You shouldn't be flattered' said Hackworth. 'That's not really the point.'

'Meaning?'

He looked a bit ill at ease.

'Maybe I can illustrate what I mean by telling you how I got involved?'

'Yes, please do.' I sat back for a lecture.

'It's slightly embarrassing' he began. 'I know I seem like an upstanding pillar of society today' … I kept a straight face …'But it wasn't always like that. To make a long story short … there wasn't much work around when I left school and I ended up doing … well … a bit of thieving. Cars. It's not something I'm proud of, but … well … '

I tried to imagine Hackworth hot-wiring BMWs, and almost smiled.

'Anyway, on this particular occasion the owner came back while I was just about to drive his Toyota away. He made a bit of a fuss …'

'Go on, Adrian.'

'Well … without really thinking about it, I broke his neck. The next thing I knew I was sitting on a metal chair being interrogated by the local police.'

An Invitation

He paused. The memory was clearly painful. 'Go on.'

'Well, the interesting thing is that a bloke in a suit turned up and sat there while the cops were reading me my rights and telling me I was looking at twenty years. Then the fuzz went out of the room and it was just him and me. He had some questions of his own …'

'Go on.'

'Long story short … he recruited me for the Department. And that's why I'm doing what I'm doing today.'

'And how does that illustrate your proposition?'

'It's what he told me. He said the Department was looking for people who seemed normal in every way but who exhibited a complete absence of moral sensibilities. He made a joke about being 'born to kill'. I think he said something about psycho-something-or-other.'

'Very interesting, Adrian. Thank you. But what's it got to do with me?'

Hackworth looked over my shoulder.

'That's exactly what they see in you.'

Major Butterworth

I left Hackworth and his 'favourite pub' with relief. There was something about him that repelled me, quite apart from his chosen calling in life.

He just didn't seem real – it was as if he'd been on a 'How to Imitate Human Beings' course. Hackworth was nothing to me – he could go to hell - but I was miffed that someone in the Department thought I was somewhat like him. What an insult!

I stomped along Vauxhall Walk feeling cross. The nerve of these people! Who did they think they were? I knew the answer. They thought they were some kind of elite ... they knew more than anyone else. They pushed and pulled the levers of power in ways that *hoi polloi* would never know about or guess.

It must be exciting to think you're so important when you're only twenty-three. Paid to lie, deceive and exploit. Close to the heart of things. Knowing what was really going on. No wonder they fancied themselves.

I plodded on in a vaguely river-wards direction, thinking grumpy thoughts and wondering if I would favour Paradise or Thai Pimlico with my custom tonight. Tricky decision. Hot and spicy or spicy and a bit hot? But my thoughts were interrupted when someone pulled gently at my arm.

'Mr McKerrell? Butterworth. I'm from Hambleside. Could I buy you a pint?'

I turned. He was a short, round person of at least sixty. He had a round face and round eyes. As if to offset this rotund effect he'd grown a severe moustache on his upper lip and across his cheeks. He looked like a Colonel Blimp cartoon. But he wasn't a joke – he clearly had a mission to perform.

Major Butterworth

Oh no. Not another Departmental goon with something important to tell me. I wanted my dinner.

'All right. If you must. Are there any good pubs round here?'

That wasn't what he had in mind. He shepherded me over the bridge and along the Embankment to the Corinthia Hotel, which I hadn't known existed. It was a bit of a trek. He was puffing and panting by the time we got there, but he seemed to think it was worth the trip. I didn't agree. This was just another big-city joint for people with money to burn.

We sat down in the bar and Butterworth slowly recovered.

I felt sorry for him. We would all be sixty one day.

'I apologise … I'm not as young as I used to be.'

'Think nothing of it! I enjoyed the walk.'

You're allowed to lie if it's good manners. You're supposed to, according to my mam.

Then I thought: 'Why on earth am I being polite?'

A waiter came up. Twenty, nervous, probably from Estonia. But I had no mercy tonight.

'Can ye gimme a middling malt from Strathclyde, laddie?' My accent wore a sporran. The boy looked stricken. The Major took over.

'I think my companion is asking to see the list of whiskies.'

'OK, Major Butterworth. You're delaying the curry I've been looking forward to all day. I don't know why, so kindly tell me and let's hope it's worth it.'

I glared at him. I wasn't a functional utensil any more. I was someone who mattered! I could be brusque! It was quite exciting. I was playing the heavy. I knew it and - damn it – I enjoyed it, but it took me only a minute to see I ought to choose a target closer to my own age and size.

Major Butterworth

Butterworth was breathless but not flustered. He had genuine good manners and began making amends.

'I'm so sorry to have waylaid you, to speak, and I'm *very* sorry to be keeping you from your Chicken Biryani, or whatever it is.'

I scowled at him. It would *never* be a Chicken Biriyani. Butterworth had obviously never travelled far from Larkhill.

The drinks arrived. I gave the waiter a big smile and a tenner. He reacted like Beaujolais when I threw him a raw steak.

Truly, these English people are strange.

But I'd felt guilty and now I didn't.

Major Butterworth was about to speak.

'I have a message for you from … well, you know.'

'Yes?' I drawled.

I was enjoying my new status, even if it was probationary.

Was I being a creep?

I could hear Father Dominic's voice. 'Not much worse but certainly no better than any other middle-aged man who feels entitled to flex his atrophied muscles thanks to some chance improvement in his circumstances.'

I moderated my tone.

'I'm sorry, Major. I've had a trying day. I don't mean to be rude. I'm hungry. Can we please cut to the chase? What are you supposed to tell me?'

'Edmonds.'

What?

'What?'

'Edmonds. You didn't know him, of course. He was, as it were, your predecessor in Prague. An accountant. Very good, they say. A marvellous facility for the Department. Very popular in the ex-pat community and well-liked among the Czechs too, as far as we can tell.'

Major Butterworth

Was I supposed to feel jealous?

'And?'

'Well, I don't know how to say this… but he was found one morning in the Vltava with his throat cut from ear to ear.'

I took a sip of Bowmore and had a quick think.

Butterworth was telling me that the guy who used to do *my* work had come to a sticky end. Was he implying that managing bank accounts for the Department could be fatal? Surely not. So … what, then?

'Do you mean that anyone connected with the Department can expect to end up in the river? Is this some weird kind of motivational campaign? *Join SIS and get killed!*'

My levity was lost on him.

'No, no, no, no. It's not that at all!'

'Well, what is it? I'm on tenterhooks.'

Butterworth didn't look at me. Didn't want to, or couldn't. Then he said, in a low voice:

'Well … it's difficult … delicate… there were suggestions … just suggestions, mind … never substantiated … that Edmonds might not have been *entirely* dedicated to the interests of the Department … if you see what I mean.'

At this point a load seemed to have been lifted from his shoulders. He looked me straight in the eye. Straightforward, military, no nonsense.

'*If you see what I mean.* I expect you do. It's all a bit sensitive, of course. No names, no pack-drill, and all that…but *they* thought someone ought to tell you about it, and … well … muggins got the job.'

'*It*' was all wrapped up in Departmental waffle and English evasion, but the message was clear. 'Do exactly what we tell you and don't get clever – or you, too, could end up as fish-food.'

Major Butterworth

Was this the usual briefing for people in my position? Or was I different? If I was different, why? I *wasn't* different, even in my own mind. Average intelligence, average business success, average lifestyle, average physical attributes. What, then?

I began to worry. Did they see something in me that I couldn't see in myself? Or was this just the usual break-test they gave to everyone earmarked for operational work?

Was I paranoid, or was there really something for me to worry about? I fell prey to dark thoughts. Were my enemies – if they existed – outside the Department, where I expected them to be, or somewhere *inside?*

Did Major Butterworth, or someone like him, waylay everyone like me and politely buy them drinks? If so, why? If not, why me?

What did I know about the notorious antipathy between MI5 and MI6? Nothing. What did I know about the structure, history or real nature of the organization I'd been working for these last ten years? Nothing.

That was the point. You didn't know anything and weren't meant to. You carried out your instructions and never asked extraneous questions.

Did I really want this job? I'd asked myself a hundred times. Father Dominic had no doubts. My real father seemed to have no doubts.

I wondered what Beaujolais would say. 'One wag for yes, two wags for no.' At this point I knew I was close to paranoia.

Perhaps a Madras at the Paradise would put everything into perspective.

It did.

A Message from Aunt Jemima

What would Fabian have to say? I soon found out.

'Aunt Jemima has had a fall. Can you meet her surgeon at the Motol University Hospital at 10.30 am tomorrow? Ask for Dr Bednar.'

I turned up at the Café Imperial ten minutes early. Fabian was already there, pretending to read the FT.

This time his hair was black and the moustache had gone. He was wearing a light-grey suit and a white shirt with a Corpus Christi Boat Club tie, which was the only element of blatant disguise I could spot today.

'Very pleased you could manage at such short notice ... awfully glad you could make it ... very good of you ... I hope this was a convenient location ... not too far off the beaten track, but not too obvious either, so to speak ... all well, I hope ...'

What?

He had never spoken to me like this before.

'I have a very pleasant duty today. A *very* pleasant duty ... a real pleasure, a *real* pleasure ... something rather special if you catch my drift. I don't want to beat around the bush, as it were. Can I go straight to the point, so to speak? Hmm?'

I couldn't be bothered any more. Too tired, too many others things on my mind. I was blunt.

'For goodness' sake, Fabian, yes. If there is one.'

Water off a duck's back.

'Happy to. More than happy to. Very, very happy to. Here .... may I?'

He handed me his copy of the Financial Times. Inside it was an envelope. Inside the envelope was a lot of cash. At a quick glance, € 40,000.

A Message from Aunt Jemima

Yay! Goodbye Volvo, Hello Porsche!

'We want you to know - that is, the Department and I – that your work in a recent ... incident ... has been noted and ... I can say... appreciated. Very much appreciated. Valuable. Very valuable. Much appreciated. Hmm?'

'But Fabian ... it was a mess. You know it was a mess. By rights it should have left the Department with egg all over its face.'

'Precisely, old chap'.

For once, Fabian had used few words.

'You know, don't you, that my kidnap idea would have been a better plan in every way. Same result, much less risk, no bloodshed, no consequences ...'

'Well ... yes ... . that point has been considered by the powers that be – at length, I might add – and ... how can I put this ... it should be construed as a factor in the modest bonus which it is my privilege and pleasure to bestow on you today ... in addition to what, I am assured, has been assessed by all concerned as a sterling performance on your part in what can only be described as extremely challenging circumstances in ... South Bohemia.. to say nothing of the very *perceptive* hint you gave us about the possible use of race-horse transporters as a covert means of smuggling weapons *and other things* across international borders...Hmm?'

I had to ask. 'And what about that useless bastard McCoig? He nearly got us all killed!'

Fabian looked slightly uncomfortable. 'Hmm. It's difficult for me to say, given my personal role and responsibilities in the Department vis-à-vis those of the operational types including the person whose name you have just mentioned. You understand, of course, that the Department functions on a strict 'need-to-know' basis... people such as whatever-his-name-is do not, as a rule, come within my purview… that said, *that said*, I can understand your feelings of – what can we say – *disappointment* – and I think I will not be going beyond my remit if I tell you that the person you refer to has received what we might call *due recompense* for his abject performance on the morning in question … hmm?'

For the first time since I had met him Fabian smiled.

I left Fabian and his looking-glass world as soon as I could, retreating to my own world of lighting-plots, rigs and gaffers. A world I knew, a world where what you saw was more or less what you got.

I decided there and then that the Department was not for me. I just didn't believe in Hackworth's zero-sum game. They win a point, we lose a point. Childish, pathetic, futile. Amoral. Tit-for-tat. Going nowhere.

I wasn't like that, whatever Hackworth and his pals thought of me. I was sensitive. I cared about other people. I liked animals. I wouldn't hurt a fly. I remembered people's birthdays. I paid my suppliers on time. I had a strong moral foundation. I knew I did.

Time passed. Galena moved out. Andrew seemed to forgive me, but couldn't resist reminding me of my awful gaffe from time to time. The other day he wore a green carnation in his lapel. The only people who knew what it meant were me and Svetlana. But it amused him, and I really couldn't blame him.

Svetlana …. oh, yes.

Domestic Bliss

'It's ready!'

Beaujolais jumped off my legs and made a bee-line for the table. I got up from the sofa and followed him. Svetlana, wearing an apron, brought steaming bowls of Green Chicken Curry through from the kitchen. Then she lit candles and we began to eat.

She was no longer Svetlana. Now she was Petra from Dubrovnik. Alasdair had given her a new identity and these days she worked for him at Stirling Security in personal protection.

'This is terrific!' Svetlana/Petra had somehow found Thai Pea Aubergines, the elusive ingredient which makes a European Thai curry resemble the real thing.

'Yum!'

She smiled happily. 'Who said the way to a man's heart is through his stomach?'

'I don't know. I'll have to ask William.'

We were living in harmony. I could damage her with a phone-call. She could destroy me with her bare hands.

Her hair was no longer red but lustrous black. She'd had a few sessions with Dr Drobny at the Perfect Person Clinic, just in case she bumped into anyone who knew her from her former life. She wore horn-rimmed glasses which made her look, in my opinion, like a pole-dancing librarian. She wore different clothes: muted trouser-suits for work and, at home – well, nothing much, really.

'How was Andrew today?'

'Oh, fine. He's forgiven me. But he still likes to twist the knife occasionally. Today, for instance, he gave me a copy of *'A Rebours'*.

'Good for him!'

Domestic Bliss

There were many things I admired about Svetlana/Petra. One of them was her familiarity with English literature. To say nothing of French, German and Russian. For a martial arts expert, she was well-read.

'And the business, Ian? I get the feeling, sometimes, that you are – well, don't take this the wrong way – perhaps a little bit bored with the movie industry...'

I looked up at her. How could she know that? Was I so transparent, or was this what used to be called 'female intuition'? Then I reminded myself of the years she'd spent at Lanark Lighting.

I began a lecture.

'It would be crazy – wouldn't it – to be tired of the most glamorous industry on the planet? But I suppose, to be honest, our role in movies is fairly humble... we provide equipment and people, but that's all we do. It's logistics. It's not creative... I sometimes think it's same-old, same-old. The challenge, if one can call it that, is just a matter of getting the right things in the right place at the right time ... we get paid fairly well, though there's no security at all ... we might get the occasional screen credit ...' At this point I was boring myself, let alone her.

I wondered if I was talking to Svetlana/Petra or myself.

'You remember that .... *thing* .... you did with those two lighting technicians in Tabor ... you know, when you came back with a hole in the top of your head?

'Y-e-e-s ... though I've been doing my best to forget it.'

'Well ... I just wondered ... if something a little more *active* might suit you better. After all, you're not *old*. You're fit and energetic.'

A few minutes later I had the chance to prove her right.

Domestic Bliss

There was an interval. I wanted to ask the questions which had been nagging at me for weeks. I didn't *really* want to because I thought I might not like the answers. But I had to.

'I have to ask … what exactly *were* you doing in Tabor?'

She raised her eyebrows and replied airily: 'Oh, just helping to make sure that someone got killed.'

That seemed to be the end of the subject. But I had another question.

'Pet … you remember that weird thing with McCoig in the ladies' loo at the office?'

'Mmm?' She put a hand on my thigh.

I pressed on. I had to.

'Well … I was just wondering … you know … how someone like you could do something like that with someone like him?'

I gritted my teeth. Did I really want to know the answer?

She sat up. An arresting sight, somewhere between the Venus de Milo and Pamela Anderson.

'Duh! That was *work*! You can be so thick sometimes, Ian!'

It was only then that I guessed what should have been obvious all along.

A Visitor

Sarka put her head round my door. 'You have a visitor!'

Sarka was my new PA. She had acquired great charm, which was a surprise to me and maybe to her.

My visitor was a man in his later years, not tall but well-built. He wore a nondescript business suit. His shoes were well-polished. His face was tanned and lined. He had dark hair, thinning in front but bushy at the back. There was a serious, no-nonsense air about him.

'Good morning – dobry den' I said. He shook my hand and sat down.

Sarka brought in coffee.

'What can I do for you?' I assumed this was a producer, or maybe a location manager, who wanted a good deal on some kind of lighting rig. We'd never seen him before, which is why Sarka brought him in to me rather than Andrew.

'You work for the British SIS, I believe.'

I just stared at him.

'Please do not be concerned. We are both, I think I can say, on the same side. The same wavelength. We have many interests in common.'

I found my tongue.

'Who exactly are you, and how can you possibly come into my office, uninvited, and make such an outrageous allegation?'

'Mr Mckerrell, Mr McKerrell … please don't be alarmed or offended. I cannot give you my name. There is a lot I know about you, but I won't say how or why. Please take it from me that we are friends.'

'I certainly *won't* take it from you! Do you think I was born yesterday?'

A Visitor

'No. You were born on the 15th November 1979 at Monklands Hospital in Airdrie. You weighed 7.5 pounds, or 3.4 kilos, if you prefer. Your father was a health-service official named James and your mother was a teacher named Mary. They are both still hale and hearty. They have an Irish setter called Scrotum. Shall I go on?'

I smothered a snigger.

'You can, but I don't see where it's going to get you. What's this about?'

'It's about someone you used to know as Svetlana but now call Petra.'

My anxiety abated. His expression was stern though well-meaning. There was no obvious threat in his face or voice. But I remained wary.

'Of course I know Petra – we live together, for goodness' sake – but what on earth has she got to do with you?'

He smiled. There was something world-weary about him, as if he had seen and done things the rest of us would never understand.

'I am happy to call her Petra. From Dubrovnik, of course.'

I just watched him and waited for what came next.

'Mr McKerrell, I simply want to say to you that Petra is *special*. She is very important to … certain interests … which are closely aligned with those of the Department you work for but which you choose to disclaim.'

'She's very special to me, too. But what exactly do you mean?'

'How can I put this? Mr Mckerrell, have you ever had a really serious argument with Petra? The kind of argument that might possibly come to blows?'

'No, I haven't. And I don't expect to.'

'Good. Good. If I may be so bold, I suggest you don't.'

154

A Visitor

He was telling me nothing new. Svetlana/Petra was fit, athletic and a martial arts expert. She'd already demonstrated her mastery of *krav maga*, or whatever it was called, by playfully putting me on my back as a prelude to… well, you know.

I began to think. What did I really know about Svetlana/Petra? Why had she appeared at Tabor on that fateful morning? What was she doing there? Was it actually Svetlana who'd dealt with four guards in seven seconds? Hackworth said so and I thought I'd recognized her in the early-morning gloom. But I didn't know.

Why was a young Czech woman a master of Excel while also being able to flip a 13-stone man on his back without even trying? Why had she acted the part of the office flirt while being – as I now knew – nothing of the sort?

But other things had happened since then. I hadn't spent much time trying to figure out the conundrum that was Svetlana/Petra.

Now I did.

My visitor sat there patiently as I slowly put it all together.

Then he smiled and got up to leave.

'Enough said, Mr McKerrell?'

Enough said.

The Appliance of Science

Vauxhall Cross didn't seem interested in my horse-transporter brainwave, so I decided on a bit of private enterprise.

I thought about it over a glass of Auchentoshan Three Wood. It occurred to me that it wasn't the transporter that mattered – how many did Sokol have? – but the horse.

What I needed was a GPS tracker which would go into Foxbat and stay there. A sugar-cube would be ideal (a Czech invention, as the whole world knew). Did such a small tracker/transponder exist?

It didn't, so I called Ondrej.

'Do you know anyone who's a whizz at miniature radio systems?'

'Funny you should ask that… as it happens, I do. She lectures in quantum mechanics at Charles University, but RF is a kind of sideline … a habit, I think you would say.'

What did he mean? Oh – 'a hobby'.

So it was that I met profesorka Zuzana Kolarova. She was not what I was expecting.

What was I expecting? The surroundings had a lot to do with it. Univerzita Karlova is an august establishment, founded in 1348 (170 years before Corpus Christi). Its Mathematics and Physics Faculty is world-class. I expected someone short, a little overweight, with glasses and hair in an untidy bun. Perhaps a pointed nose. But that's not what greeted me in reception.

The professor was my height and slender. She had an oval, intelligent face and a small nose. Her eyes were large and almond-shaped. No glasses. Her hair was chestnut, worn loose round her shoulders. Her clothes were practical: a green two-piece suit.

The Appliance of Science

She had said something and I'd missed it.

'Hello, Mr McKerrell' she repeated. 'Welcome to our university.'

'I'm so sorry. I lost track there for a moment.'

'Perhaps I am not exactly what you were expecting?'

She led me down a corridor lined with offices. Opening a door, she waited for me to go in first. I waited for her to go in first.

'Please, Mr McKerrell. I am the host, you are the guest. After you.'

I did what I was told, reflecting that the film industry was years behind the world of academia when it came to etiquette. When I realised I'd put 'film industry' and 'etiquette' in the same sentence I smiled.

'Is it funny?' asked the *profesorka*.

'No, no … not at all… it's just that I work in a fairly traditional area, so … well, I'm just a bit behind the times, I suppose.'

She didn't think it was funny.

'Welcome to the 21st century, Mr McKerrell.'

This was not a good start. How could I win her co-operation?

I sat down and she poured tea at a table by the window. Outside I could see the trunk of a giant Wych elm, one of the few to have survived the epidemic. I commented on it.

Her face lit up.

'Yes! We are so lucky! Ninety per cent of our elms died from *ophiostoma*. You probably know it as vascular wilt. This one is nearly two hundred years old. We have done everything we can think of to protect it. Trees mean so much to us here. I love them. You too?'

For once I could be honest.

The Appliance of Science

'Very much so. Where I grew up it was nearly all pine and birch, so I've been impressed by the variety of deciduous trees you have here and the way you look after them.'

It worked. We could be friends again.

'Ondrej says you have an interesting problem ... a GPS tracking device?'

'Yes, I do. He says you are the only person in Europe who could solve it for me.'

That worked, too. I don't care who you are, there's no-one on Earth immune to flattery. As long as it's applied with a palette-knife, not a trowel.

'Perhaps I could explain?'

I'd made up a story about horse-thieves. I wanted to be able to locate my gelding 'Lancer' if a gang kidnapped him or hi-jacked his horse-box.

'So it's like the trackers that people attach to their dogs and cats?'

'Kind of ... except this one has to be invisible, so it's got to be internal. I was thinking of a sugar-lump.'

She thought about this, then went to her desk and started tapping keys. She put on a pair of wire-rimmed glasses.

'What kind of range do you need?'

'I think 20 km should be enough. But – I don't really know what I'm talking about, so forgive my ignorance – can the unit be designed to respond rather than transmit? To keep power consumption to a minimum?'

She looked at me, taking her glasses off.

'Yes, Mr McKerrell, it can. You seem to have thought this out.'

'Not really. Just the basic idea.'

The Appliance of Science

'It will have to be specially-made, of course. And we have to think how to make sure it lodges securely somewhere in the horse's digestive tract.'

I'd thought about this too, but considered it too indelicate to mention.

'I have a colleague, Dr Merunka, who's an expert on equine anatomy. I can ask him.'

We spoke briefly about fees. Something for the professor and a donation to the university's linear accelerator fund. As with most things in the Czech Republic, good value at the price.

'It's nearly time for lunch. I'm going to a small restaurant in Albertov. Would you care to join me?'

A month ago I'd been dumped by Galena and thought it was all over. Now I had the fascinating, intimidating Svetlana/Petra living in my flat, undisguised interest from Katerina Sokol, and a lunch invitation from this strange hybrid of model-girl and Nobel Prize-winner. What was happening?

Was it my money? No, I was comfortable but nothing more. Was it my looks? No, very unlikely. I was no Alasdair or Andrew. Could it be my scintillating conversation? Doubtful. Was it my aura of high moral purpose and rock-like inner strength?

Yes, I decided. That must be it.

But I was wrong. It was The Movies, yet again.

We walked down Albertov to the Bistro Bohemia, where we were given a table in the window. The professor was obviously a valued customer.

'May I call you Ian?'

'Of course... and may I call you Prof?'

She laughed.

'*No!* It makes me think of Velma. My name is Zuzana.'

The Appliance of Science

'Very well... though I have to warn you that my own understanding of science is so minimal that you'll probably get up and leave in disgust.'

'But why should you know *anything* about science unless you have studied it? We can't know everything these days. The last person who did was Thomas Young, and he died in 1829. Unless you're OpenAI. Are you?'

I had no idea how to answer, but it didn't matter. The waiter arrived and we ordered. Zuzana gave me the wine-list. Some conventions die hard.

'Now. Ondrej says you work in film production up at Barrandov.'

'Yes, I do. We have a lighting company and we rig the lights for some of the productions made here in Prague.'

'How exciting! So do you get to meet the stars?'

'Yes, I do. Once they are 'stars' they're very particular about how they want to be lit. You can see why – looks are a matter of life or death when your face is 7 metres by 3 metres and watched by 500 people at once. Most actors prefer multiplex and home video. It's more forgiving.'

She seemed puzzled.

'But why? Surely what you see is more or less what's really there?'

This could be a long answer. I took a swig of Vermentino.

'Have you looked at any influencers lately?'

'Yes... though it's not a big thing for me...'

Of course not.

'So you'll be aware that they way they appear on your device is nothing like how they look in reality? You know they use a hundred optical tricks to seem bigger, smaller, more beautiful, more handsome, thinner, tougher, sexier, more soulful, harder, softer, older, younger... than they are in real life?'

The Appliance of Science

'I suppose so. Now I come to think about it.'

'OK. Well, the movie industry has been doing *exactly* the same thing, using very similar optical illusions, since 1920. Clever lighting is one of them, and that's where people like us come in.'

If I had expected to dampen her enthusiasm I was wrong.

'How absolutely fascinating! So you actually *talk* to people like Russell Crowe?'

I remembered the last time. I'd managed to blot it out of my memory until now.

'Yes, we do.'

What was the point? Zuzana was an expert in quantum mechanics – whatever that was – but when it came to Hollywood she was just like everyone else. I reflected, yet again, that movies and football somehow transcended all human divisions – ethnic, tribal, nationalistic, religious, cultural. Why hadn't the UN noticed?

'I don't suppose …'

I knew what was coming.

'Of course, Zuzana. It would be a great pleasure.'

As it turned out it was, but not in the way I'd expected.

Her Story

I needed to know. She was perfect in so many ways, but she was a *matryoshka*. It had been a long time since I thought women could be 'understood'. I'd watched my mam rule the roost for years while letting my dad think he was Master of The House. I knew that women figured things out in ways that men couldn't. I had a sneaking suspicion that women were usually in charge, and probably had been since the Minoans.

But this wasn't just *vive la différence*. This was a gap in my understanding that could threaten Lanark Lighting or – much worse – the Department. I knew almost nothing about Svetlana/Petra.

I would have to confront her.

Minoans ... I took the bull by the horns.

We had just finished dinner, a very good Nasi Goreng (though I say it myself).

'Milacku ... I was thinking ... here we are, living together and very happy ... at least, I hope that's how you feel ... but the thing is ... the truth is ...I don't really know anything much about you. Do you see what I mean?'

Not great, but a start.

'Yes, of course I see what you mean. After all, we have only known each other since Lanark Lighting was working on supermarket commercials.'

Was that a pout?

'No, no – please don't misunderstand! I love you to bits, you know I do. I've never been so happy in my whole life. I can't imagine being with anyone else, ever...'

I was no good at saying the things that women like to hear. Never had been. I just didn't have Alasdair's gifts. But I blundered on.

Her Story

'The point is, Pet ... well, you know I'm involved in a very small way with – what can I call it – *government business* ... and – well – I'm just a bit scared that I know so little – nothing, really – about who you are, where you come from and.. well ...'

I had run out of words.

She looked at me in a way that can only be described as kindly. There was a long pause. Then she spoke.

'Ian. Do you love me?'

'What? Yes, of course I do. Completely. Absolutely. Totally.'

'Good. I will tick that box. Next: can you imagine spending the rest of your life with me?'

'Yes! Yes! That's exactly what I want to happen!'

'Good. I can tick that box, too. Next: do you trust me?'

I had to think. Can you trust someone you know next-to-nothing about? Or was it more a matter of instinct? I really didn't know, so I blathered.

'Yes! I think so. Or – how can I put it – I *feel* I can trust you, even though I don't really know the first thing about you. But that's exactly the point I'm trying to make!'

'OK. Half a tick in that box. Now: why *exactly* do you want to know all these facts about me that are not in my Lanark Lighting personnel file?'

She smiled and raised her eyebrows in the way she *knew* got me every time. She crossed her legs – same effect. Then she tossed her hair back, and I was lost.

'Not bad, Mr McKerrell. Now let me see ... you have scored 80 per cent on the Cosmo fidelity test. Not 100 per cent, but a lot better than average. She looked at me again. There was something about her eyes which turned my knees to jelly. What colour were they? Very dark, almost black, but a trace of – what was it? Violet?

Her Story

'You have passed the test, so I will now tell you my story.'

I couldn't move or say a word.

'You have to imagine a small village in the depths of the country then called Czechoslovakia. I was an orphan, living with a family who made a bare living from their smallholding. They sold some of their crops on the black market to get by, so we all had just about enough to eat. But it was very basic. The roof leaked, it was cold at night, we could never see further than a week or two ahead. Even so, it was a happy household.

I didn't know I was an orphan. I thought my brothers and sister were the same as me. Why not? Children don't ask these questions. One day, when I was twelve, I had to. My mother took me to one side and told me that my real parents had been executed by the government – though she didn't say it quite like that – and I was a foster-child.'

I tried to imagine this, and couldn't.

'I wanted to know why – obviously – but my foster-mother, who was a good woman, didn't want to tell me. In the end she was forced to admit that it was because they had been Jews. Then I realised, of course, that I was also a Jew, and only alive because of the good nature of the family who had taken me in and brought me up alongside their own children.'

Her face was expressionless as she told me this. I was shocked. I knew something about anti-semitism in Central Europe. The ghastly story of the Nazis' extermination programme was vivid and inescapable. But I had never encountered it face-to-face. Until now.

'As I grew up I learnt more about what it meant to be Jewish in the region where I lived. I tried to find out about the fate of my parents, but in those days it was all buried deep in

Her Story

government archives – for good reason. When I was eighteen I decided that I had to act. You know what I mean by *act*?'

'Not really.'

'Dear Ian, such things have never happened to you and – God willing - they never will. But please imagine an 18-year-old girl who is strong, smart and capable. She realizes that a terrible crime has been committed against her parents and, if your mind can stretch that far, against her whole people, race, religion, nation ... call it what you will.

I had to act. I *had* to.

I bade farewell to my foster-family and made my way to Israel. I was one of many thousands, mostly – at that time – from Russia. You can imagine ... there was some tension between us. But there was – how do you say it in English ? – a *higher cause* which united us. Survival. We would *not* be extinguished by the hatred and jealousy of people who'd been our neighbours and pretended to be our friends. We would fight back. We would survive. It's really as simple as that.'

I tried to work this out. Svetlana/Petra had gone to Israel, like so many others, to do her bit. She was clever, good-looking and fit. She could have harvested olives on a farm or been a flight attendant with El Al. She could have applied her brain to the IDF's cyber-war programme. Anything. So what had happened?

'Can I ask ... what happened to make you what you are – whatever that is – in Prague, of all places?'

'It's simple. I met a man who made me an offer – suggestion is perhaps a better word. It led to this.'

'*You met a man*? Really? How? Where?'

'In a bar. Don't look so surprised. How did SIS recruit *you*? How? Where?'

She had me. It *was* in a bar. Touche.

Her Story

'You've spoken with him. He thought you were OK. Nothing special, but OK.' She smirked.

'Right ... so – let me make sure I've got this straight ... ever since you arrived back in the Czech Republic you've been an agent for one of the Israeli secret services ... Aman, Shin Bet, Mossad?'

Another smirk.

'Fine! I'm absolutely fine with this! I just wanted to know where I stood! Petra, I'm right behind you!'

'Mmm. That's exactly what I'd hoped.'

She grabbed my hand and led me into the bedroom, where I realised that she was also a dab hand at innuendo.

A Drink with Alasdair

Alasdair peered at my face. 'Yes – almost back to normal. At least, what passes for normal in your case.'

I expected nothing less from Alasdair. We'd been friends for years, two Scotsmen who'd somehow ended up in Prague, but our roles were clearly assigned. He was the head-turner – the women in our office called him 'Your friend the matinee idol', and I was – well – not.

It didn't matter to me. I'd never turned heads and couldn't imagine what it was like. But no complaints. At the same time, I wondered if Alasdair's Colin Firth looks were why he seemed to have dozens of girlfriends but very few mates.

Then again, he was a lifelong Hibs supporter. That could be it.

'Nice to see you, and thanks for the morale-boost.'

'What did you expect? The day I say something nice to you is the day you need to keep your back to the wall. Like with Andrew.' There was a sound like a donkey braying. Alasdair was laughing.

How on earth had he heard about that? Someone must have talked. It could only be Andrew himself.

'I didn't know you and Andrew were acquainted.'

'Oh, aye. We've been meeting for the odd drink ever since he started working for you. Best way to keep tabs. Anyway, he was a Marine – good type. When he's fed up with you movie-luvvies he can come straight over to SSS.'

'That'll be the day. You're the living embodiment of everything we movie-luvvies can't stand. Though opinions are divided on Sean Connery.'

Alasdair had traditional views. He was a Unionist, but not because he thought Scotland needed England. It was the other

A Drink with Alasdair

way round. He thought Scotland was the dog wagging the English tail. He could prove it, and often did over two or three hours of history lectures, starting with the Picts. This meant a lot of Kozel followed by a malt night-cap, so I put up with them.

'How's business – if you can tell me?' I enquired.

'Oh, not so bad.' From Alasdair, or any other Scotsman, this was enough to make you phone in a 'buy' order. It was part of his temperament to talk things down.

Alasdair's life had followed a curious pattern. He'd been born and brought up in Stirling, a historic city which had seen better days. He could have taken his pick of the universities but chose instead to join the Highland Light Infantry as an enlisted man. He was invited to go for a commission but didn't like that idea and quit, spending the next few years as a 'soldier of fortune' in the Middle East and South-East Asia.

In his thirties he fetched up in Prague and began providing security personnel to companies, buildings and individuals who felt they needed protection. It turned out to be a growing market and Stirling Security Services soon made a name for itself. Alasdair was earning a lot of money but would never admit it.

'Not so bad. Could be better, of course'.

'Alasdair ... I wanted to thank you for what you did for Petra.'

'Don't be daft! It was just business! She's one of the best-qualified close protection operatives I've ever had the pleasure of meeting. The best part is that she *looks* as if she couldn't take the top off a Coke-bottle.'

'I know, I know. I knew that's what you'd say. But the fact remains, we're both indebted to you. We're very grateful. You

A Drink with Alasdair

very possibly saved her life, and that matters to me for obvious reasons.'

Alasdair didn't like this kind of talk. He called it 'wishy-washy'. But I had to say it. Petra and I had been in a difficult situation, to put it mildly, until Alasdair waved his magic wand. I wanted to express my gratitude. With Alasdair, there was only one way.

'I know – shall we do chasers tonight?'

His eyes lit up. 'Yes! But let me just check what I've got on tomorrow.'

He looked at his phone.

'It's fine. We're taking care of Pavel Cerny. He's speaking at a conference, but the only person *he's* got to worry about is his wife.'

'Great!' I looked up and the waiter was there in seconds.

'The thing is, Alasdair …'

His eyebrows were raised in polite enquiry. Like many Scotsmen, he either said a lot or nothing at all.

'The thing is …. well, you know that … *incident* … down in South Bohemia … you, know, when Stepan Sokol drowned?'

Alasdair nodded.

'Well … I've had a suggestion from some people in London and I'm not quite sure what to make of it.'

'Let me guess. They think you've got what it takes and they want you to go operational?'

I gawped at him.

'They liked what you did in a badly-organised, badly-conducted operation and they think you may have abilities which are, to say the least, rare among their usual type of recruit.'

How did he know anything about the Tabor fiasco? Or the Department? But I was being dim. In Alasdair's line of work you needed connections all over the place. He was very likely

A Drink with Alasdair

a confidant of Sir Reginald Handiside. They probably had drinks at the Special Forces Club.

In any case, what Hackworth had hinted at was much more Alasdair's world than mine. Physical action, weapons, danger ... not bulbs, lenses and electricians. Whatever he had to say was worth hearing

'OK, thou all-knowing guru. I beseech thee for thy wise counsel.' (This was after three beers).

'It's either complicated or simple.'

'Yes ... and?'

'Let's start with the complicated version. You're a man in – let's say – the prime of life. You've built up a successful business which gives you a decent income. Your personal affairs are a bit of a mess ...'

He held up his hand to stop me interrupting.

'But that's par for the course these days, and in any case it looks as if you may – I only say *may* – have found, at long last, the right partner in life ...

And you have a dog'.

I had been nodding to show that I was following his argument, but at this point I had to stop him.

'Dog? What's Beaujolais got to do with my career?'

'Ah'. He tapped his nose. 'You don't know, but it doesn't matter.'

He continued with the *complicated version.*

'You have, let's say, ten years of active life ahead of you before beginning that long, slow decline into golf, bridge and local politics.'

I stared at him. This was a bit near the knuckle.

'The complicated solution is finding a new meaning in life ... it could be love, and in your case it certainly is ... but we both know how long the flame of ardour burns, don't we?'

A Drink with Alasdair

I could have said something witty about ardour, flames and Alasdair, but I kept my peace.

'I think you get the point. You might be from Lanark and a Hearts supporter, but you're not completely stupid.' He grinned happily. 'From our point of view you're practically English. But we'll let bygones be bygones. You lost, after all.'

I said nothing. It was usually worth enduring a barrage of mild insults to get the advice I wanted.

'Then there's the simple version.'

'Yes, please'.

'Right. Your life is boring but you've *accidentally* had an experience which set your pulse racing and made you feel truly alive after so many years of mere existence. Correct?'

'Um … yes, I suppose so.'

'Well – it's blindingly obvious, isn't it? You've got a simple choice, Mr McKerrell. Thrills, risk, adventure, danger … or bridge.'

I said nothing. I didn't need to, because Alasdair went off on one of his 'Scots are different, Scots are best' diatribes. I zoned out, thinking about what he'd said. When I started listening again he was up to James Clerk Maxwell, and I had no idea what he was talking about.

He was right. I had a clear choice. I needed to decide. A comfortable existence, descending imperceptibly into quiet, irrelevant old age? Or a jump into the unknown, with all the pain and problems that might entail? I wondered what Petra would say, and I knew there was only one answer to Alasdair's question.

It was time to interrupt the lecture. In for a penny, in for a pound.

A Drink with Alasdair

'So, Ali … I've been thinking about our home towns. You know they call Dundee 'The City of the Three Js' – Jute, Jam and Journalism?.

'Of course I do.'

'I was thinking about Stirling. It's difficult, but let me tell you what I've come up with. It's the City of the Three Ws – Wallace, Woo-hoo and Wa … people like you!'

He didn't much like this, and wasn't meant to. He glowered. Then:

'All right, what about glorious Lanark? I've been racking my brains, and I think I've got it.

'And…?'

'The Three Ns – Nothing, Nothing and Nothing!'

'Walter Smith!'

'Billy Bremner!'

It was time to up the ante.

'As for your heroes … Robert the Bruce wasn't even Scottish. He came from Bruges! And William Wallace … he spent half his life fighting for the English. Where do you think he got his money from? He was no more a Highland hero than you are!'

It worked. This was too much. With a growl Alasdair stood up, leaned across the table and grabbed me by the collar.

Within seconds two large men appeared from nowhere and put us out in the street, deftly relieving us of what we owed on our way through the door. They were used to guests from the British Isles at The Dublin Golem.

Alasdair couldn't have been happier. 'Hah! You bampot!'

It was all my fault, of course.

'Can you not have a quiet jar without getting the StB involved? Come on now - where next?'

Andrew's Future

Andrew came into my room.

'We need to talk.'

'Of course, Andrew. Whatever, whenever you like.'

'I've been doing some thinking.'

'Oh …?'

'Yes. There are certain things about Lanark Lighting – and you, if I'm honest – which don't add up.'

'What kind of things?'

'Well, for a start, those two goons you brought in to work on Gideon's commercial. They were no more lighting technicians than I'm Yuri Gagarin. So what were they really?'

I couldn't tell him, so I flannelled.

'Oh, just a couple of chaps Alasdair hired … needed a bit of cover … only too happy to oblige, you know the kind of thing …'

'Yes, I knew you'd say that, but I asked Alasdair and he'd never heard of them. So I'll ask you again: who or what were they really?'

I was trapped. If Andrew was going to be the future of Lanark Lighting he needed to trust me implicitly. I could see that his confidence was on a knife-edge. I would have to come clean.

'OK. You've signed the Official Secrets Act, I take it?'

'Yes. Of course.'

'Right. Well … how can I explain this … it's all a bit delicate …years ago I started doing odds and ends for HMG types who wanted things like shell companies set up, money moved around, cover-stories constructed … that sort of stuff … all in aid of the intelligence work that used to be so important here in Prague …'

Andrew's Future

Andrew was on the edge of his chair.

'And is again today.'

'Exactly. Now things are moving into higher gear, for obvious reasons. Those two 'goons' as you describe them – and, by the way, I couldn't agree more – were sent here to carry out a particular mission which was ultra, ultra secret and must never see the light of day.'

'Wow! You mean …'

'Yes. I, and you, and Lanark Lighting are involved, in a small way, in assisting the British government with geopolitical activities which are both super-important and super-secret. I'm sorry, I probably ought to have told you. I would have, in due course, but I was … waiting for the right moment …'

Andrew's eyes were shining.

'What – really? Lanark Lighting is mixed up with spooks? John Le Carre and all that? *Really*?'

'Well, yes … though it's nothing like as exciting as it is in books and films … mainly fairly humdrum work, making arrangements, providing resources … a bit like supplying lighting to the studios, now I come to think of it.'

But my monotonous explanation wasn't working.

'Wow!' said Andrew. 'That's the best news in years! *You* might not find it exciting, but *I* do! Right! You can rely on me to run Lanark Lighting for you from here to eternity – on one condition.'

'What's that?'

'I want in.'

I thought about this for all of five seconds. It was the answer to a prayer.

Petra's Lesson

We'd had a very good Beef Redang at Shrimi in Arbesovo namesti and were wandering home. As we walked up Elisky Peskove I spotted four young men coming in the opposite direction. They were making the farmyard noise which indicates drunk Brits anywhere on the planet.

As we came closer the four spread out to block the pavement. I'd been to Glasgow, so I knew what this meant. So, it seemed, did Petra. 'Hold this', she said, giving me her handbag.

She walked ahead of me and stopped in front of the four louts, who failed to understand what was happening. They mooed and jeered, shifting to surround her. No-one even looked in my direction.

'Now, boys, we don't want any trouble, do we?' said Petra in a low voice. She stood quite still, relaxed, with her arms at her sides.

'No, we don't. And there won't fuckin' be any. We're out for a bit of fun, and it looks like you're it!'

'Are you sure?'

One of them reached forward to grab Petra's arm.

I'm not certain what happened next. It was a blur. In the blink of an eye all four were lying on the pavement. One was throwing up on his shoes, one was clutching his groin and moaning. Two were silent and motionless.

Petra retrieved her handbag. 'How annoying' she said, with a slight frown.

When we reached home I got out the brandy – I needed one – and said: 'How did you do that?'

'Oh, it was nothing, really'. Petra's eyes twinkled.

For me it had been a fresh underpants situation. For her it had been mildly amusing.

Petra's Lesson

'But what exactly did you do? I couldn't see – it was all too quick.'

'Well, milacku, that's the whole point, really.'

'What do you mean?'

'Ian – have you *ever* had a real fight?'

I thought back. Nothing came to mind. There'd been the usual pushing and shoving, plenty of 'Want some of this, dickhead' when I was growing up in Lanark. But I'd always managed to make myself scarce or talk my way out of it. 'He who doesn't fight and runs away, lives to fight another day.' My mam knew a thing or two.

'Not really.'

'I think I can see why. But in my book that makes you a wise man among fools. Let's keep it that way.'.

She smiled sweetly.

'But hang on a minute … I can't go through the rest of my life being defended by a nine-stone woman!'

'Why not?'

I didn't have a ready answer. Why not, indeed?

'Because … because … well, it's obvious, isn't it? I'm a man and *I'm* supposed to protect *you*, not the other way round!'

Arched eyebrows.

'Whatever gave you that idea?'

'History … evolution … culture … literature … men are bigger and stronger … we open doors for you … we walk on the kerb-side of the pavement so your clothes don't get splashed – unless, of course, this would mean our swords getting tangled up in your crinolines … oh, I don't know, it's just the way it is! It always has been!'

Petra burst out laughing.

Petra's Lesson

'I love it! I love it! I thought I'd got myself a lighting technician who can cook and what I've actually got is a throwback! Ian, where have you been for the last forty years?'

Did she have a point? Had things changed so much? Well, yes, probably, if tonight's episode was anything to go by.

'OK. You win. I'm behind the times. But you *knew* that.'

'Yes, I knew that' she said gently.

'All right. But please tell me … what *did* you do in Elisky Peskove?'

'You really want to know?'

'Yes, I *really* want to know. I want to keep my end up … carry my weight … you know what I mean … . I want to be there, in it, not standing like a loon holding his girlfriend's handbag!'

Petra told me.

'It's mainly about surprise. You've got to make them think they have the upper hand. This means their guard is down. The more vulnerable and harmless you look, and the more puffed-up they are with their own superiority, the bigger your advantage.'

'Yes, I saw you do that this evening. It certainly worked. But isn't that Rule One in military strategy from Alexander to Napoleon?'

'Yes, of course it is. But you'll notice that most amateur street-fighters do the opposite. They like to shout and posture. This is a sure sign they're pretending to be confident when they're not really.'

'Ahah. So – quiet, calm, unthreatening. Got that. What next?'

'Take the initiative. Act! Hit hard, fast and first. You have to forget all about your Queensferry Rules.'

'Queensberry Rules'.

Petra's Lesson

'Whatever. Do you get the point? You've got to learn how to wind your energy up to an explosive level without a *trace* of it showing.'

'That sounds difficult. But you did it, so it can't be *that* difficult!'

'Oh, Ian. Stop giggling. How old are you?'

'Sorry.'

'You won't like this, but you have to be super-fit.'

She glanced at my midriff and covered her mouth with her hand.

'That's nothing! Nothing! A couple of sessions in Jim's Gym and I'll be back to fighting form! It's genetic. I've got *fit genes*.'

The eyebrows again. Then she continued.

'Now, if you've got that, it's all a question of *what* to do. This is where you really have to learn some techniques … and a bit about anatomy.'

'Anatomy? What's that got to do with the price of fish?'

'Fish?'

'What I mean is … what's anatomy got to do with mortal combat?'

'Ah. Well, a lot. There are certain parts of the body where a small amount of force can have a devastating effect.'

I leered. 'That's *not* what I mean!' said Petra.

'Sorry. Please go on.'

'You just have to learn this stuff. For instance: a sharp blow at the base of the nose, in a diagonal upward direction, can drive splinters of bone into your opponent's brain… and the fight is over. You need to learn this… and then you need to learn how to apply force and leverage without being a 100-kilo WMAC champion.'

'Yes! This is just what I need to know. Where can I find it?'

Petra's Lesson

'Well … I'm sorry to disappoint you but you won't find it in books. There's a bit on the web, but mostly half-cooked. The authorities try to keep close-combat techniques well away from Tom, Dick and Jerry.'

'Harry.'

She gave me a look. 'I'll try to believe you're just trying to improve my colloquial English. But you'll have to stop sniggering like a schoolboy. Try to act like a *schoolmaster* instead.'

This gave me an idea. Petra seemed to have the same idea. We drained our glasses and rushed into the bedroom.

Pencak Silat

'Milacku, what's wrong?'

Was it so obvious? I was sitting in my G-Plan armchair, nursing a glass of Glen Moray. Petra was getting dinner ready. I was moping, but I didn't think it showed.

'Oh ... nothing really ... just contemplating things generally ... you know.'

I gave a weak smile.

'Come on now, Ian. Tell Auntie Petra!'

'It's really nothing. Really.'

'Ian!'

'OK. If you insist. It's just that I'm feeling a bit ... I don't know ... *ineffective*. I don't want to be a handbag-holder all my life.'

I'd said it. There was no point holding out on Petra. And it was true. In my mind's eye I was still the fighter-pilot hero of my boyhood dreams. It had been a shock to stand by and watch while this slip of a girl demolished four louts in ten seconds.

Petra stroked my hair.

'You can be very silly sometimes. I've *told* you it doesn't matter.'

'Maybe not to you. But it does to me. I'm a man and I'm supposed to do manly things. I'm sorry, Pet, but I can't change the way I was brought up.'

'Can't you? I think you can, and I think you should. It would make you a lot happier. It would make *me* a lot happier.'

'It's hard to explain. Dyed in the wool, bred in the bone ... it's evolution. I'm meant to go out hunting dangerous animals with the other chaps while you collect berries and dig up roots ... I can't help it.'

Pencak Silat

I looked at her sideways She raised her eyes to heaven.

'OK, OK. I hear what you say. It's not enough to be an expert in the marital arts – you want to be a martial arts expert too.'

I put on my Labrador face. It worked.

'OK. This stuff takes years to learn, but you're right. It's never too late to start. If it *really* bothers you I'll see what I can do.'

'You can? You will? Yes please.'

That was Tuesday. On Wednesday Petra advised me to do some running and limbering-up exercises. On Friday she took me to an Indonesian martial arts class at the kick-boxing gym in Stefanikova.

'We ought to be starting with the absolute basics, but I know you. You haven't got the patience. So we're going to begin with mid-level Pencak Silat.'

'Pencak what?'

'Silat. It's an Indonesian combat system which has been developed over a thousand years. They think of it as an art-form, and it is, with all kinds of philosophical and cultural implications. But you don't need to worry about that. All you need to learn is how to break a few bones.'

'Will it hurt?'

She thought for a moment.

'Yes, it's painful. *Obviously*. But you won't get injured.'

'Oh, good. Why aren't I learning Krav Magna?'

'Krav Maga? Because then you *would* get injured, and I prefer you fit, healthy and fully capable of performing your domestic duties.'

She was right. Was I making a mistake? Was my male pride leading me to a humiliating fall? Oh well, I'd soon find out.

Pencak Silat

We entered the gym and were greeted by a short individual with a big smile. He was wearing a black tunic and loose trousers. Bare feet.

'*Selamat datang! Vitejte*! Welcome!'

Petra told me I was about to receive a special, one-on-one 'Senior Seminar' from Tarimin, the visiting Pencak Silat instructor.

'Is that senior as in *very important*, or senior as in *old*?'

'Whatever makes you happy.'

Tarimin led me off to change. He walked like a leopard. I began to feel apprehensive. On the other hand, perhaps I, too, would move like a feral cat after a couple of Pencak Silat lessons …

We came back to the neoprene mat.

'Warm-up routine, please!' said Tarimin.

It was embarrassing. They were both watching me. I did my best to look as if this was something I did every day.

'Right', said Tarimin. 'Please attack me.'

I turned sideways and advanced menacingly, left hand outstretched and fingers spread. I took small steps, keeping my weight evenly balanced, knees bent. I had read the books, checked the websites and seen the films. I knew what to do.

Tarimin didn't seem to do anything at all.

Whump!

I was flat on my back with an excruciating pain in my lower spine. It was like Petra's Krav Maga lesson but much faster and ten times worse.

Tarimin reached down and helped me back on my feet.

'May I please explain what I did? In slow motion?'

He demonstrated. He really hadn't done very much at all. A step, a turn, his right arm *here* and his left arm *there*. All the energy was what I brought with me.

Pencak Silat

It seemed very simple.

'Now, you try, please.'

Tarimin came towards me. I took a step and turned. I wrapped my right arm round his neck, as he had shown me.

Nothing happened. It was as if he was bolted to the floor.

'Yes, I see what's wrong', he said. 'The timing is very important.'

He went through it again. I watched carefully. There were so many things to get right, all at the same time.

I realised this kind of balance and co-ordination wasn't something you could acquire in a couple of lessons. I would not be a leopard. Maybe a capybara.

We tried again. And again. This went on for an hour.

Out of the corner of my eye I could see Petra giggling.

I had to admit defeat. I couldn't shift him. But he could throw me without even trying. It was frustrating. At the same time, I was impressed. I wondered how the Vikings would have fared if they'd ever made it to Southeast Asia.

Tarimin seemed disappointed. He'd evidently hoped for more progress. Maybe I was *too senior*.

I got changed, we shook hands and Tarimin gave me his card 'in case I was ever in Medan'. I had learnt one useful lesson today. Never, for any reason, on any account, would I willingly visit the home of Pencak Silat.

On the way back Petra gave me her handbag. I almost took it, but she'd doubled up in helpless mirth. It was a Petra joke.

A Dinner Invitation

Alasdair invited me and Petra to dinner. This was a first. In all the years I'd known him I'd never been inside his flat. We knew every pub in Prague and were still welcome in most of them, but we'd only ever met on neutral territory.

I wondered what was going on.

Beaujolais was staying home, so he got extra Winalot. Petra bought flowers, I bought a bottle of Talisker and we turned up at Kajatanka exactly five minutes late. Alasdair greeted us at the door in a kilt.

Petra couldn't resist. She flipped it up and had a good look. 'I've always wanted to know!' she squeaked.

Alasdair took this in his stride. It probably wasn't the first time, or the thirtieth. 'About me, you mean, or Scotsmen in general?'

He guided us through to the sitting-room. It wasn't what I'd expected.

No guns or military bric-a-brac. Instead, tapestries and paintings that even I could recognize as Renaissance. A Corinthian helmet. A devil-mask from Papua New Guinea. A Gothic statue which must have been looted in the Thirty Years War. A Shakespeare folio open on a lectern, and on another a King James Bible. I noticed that everything was artfully lit. Now I knew what Alasdair did with his money. It was like a museum. Clearly, the man had secrets. But I didn't know the half of it.

He sat us down and opened a bottle of Roederer Cristal. 'I hope you like this stuff?' he enquired.

Petra made a silly face. I nodded.

'A that moment a voice said: 'Hi, you two! Welcome!'

It was Andrew, wearing a tartan apron.

A Dinner Invitation

He shook my hand and kissed Petra, who kissed him back warmly. I hadn't been entirely wrong. They were obviously on very good terms.

We all raised our glasses. 'Here's tae us!'

'We've got something to tell you.'

I guessed what was coming, but I was still trying to adjust all sorts of ideas and assumptions which had ruled my notion of Alasdair for years.

'As you can see …'

'Yes, it's pretty obvious. The thing is, Ali, I always thought … well, you know, all the girls and macho stuff … I just had no idea. No idea at all. I was completely taken in'

Petra interrupted. 'I wasn't. I *always* knew.'

I glanced at her. A complacent smile. Was I really so dim? Yes, apparently I was. I'd got Petra wrong, Andrew wrong and *Alasdair* wrong – someone I'd known for ages.

'So *some* of us movie-luvvies make the grade, do we?'

Alasdair gave me a wry grin. I felt like a fool.

My feelings didn't matter. Alasdair and Andrew were obviously made for each other. Petra and me … well, I hoped so.

I proposed a toast: 'To the two happy couples!'

We went through to dinner. I was still slightly shell-shocked. My three companions – conspirators, as I now thought of them – were enjoying my discomfort. But that all faded away when Andrew produced one of the best Beef Wellingtons I'd ever seen.

Over brandy I felt entitled to ask a few questions.

'Why?'

'You have to bear in mind when I was born, where I was born and the work I did for most of my life. It was simply *necessary* to create a façade. I wasn't the only one. But women

A Dinner Invitation

seemed to like me, so it was probably a lot easier for me than it was for many others.'

'How?'

'Acting, dear boy!' said Alasdair in the voice of John Gielgud.

'OK... and why didn't I guess?'

Petra chimed in. 'You work for British Intelligence, don't you?'

'Yes, I think I can admit to that between these four walls.

'Enough said, then.'

Everyone laughed.

More brandy. Alasdair came to sit beside me. 'No hard feelings, I hope, Ian?' he said. Then he put his hand on my knee.

My face must have been a picture, because everyone suddenly fell about laughing.

'None, Ali, none at all. In fact, I couldn't be happier.'

I meant it. Alasdair and Andrew were happy, Petra and I were happy. What more could I want?

Then I remembered what Ali had said about bridge. There were four of us here, and I was the dummy.

Oh, well.

Heroes

My phone rang. Unknown number. Could be new business. 'Hello. Lanark Lighting, McKerrell speaking.'

'Oh, hello Mr McKerrell. I'm David DeVere. I'm from … London. I wondered if you might have a spare hour for a bit of a chat?'

'Are you selling something?'

I didn't mind if he was, but I liked sales-pitches to be sales-pitches, minus all the flim-flam some of these people thought necessary.

'No, I'm not. It's not like that. I'm in Prague and I just wanted to talk to you about … I'm not sure how to put it. *Vauxhall.*'

Ah. Now I knew.

'Of course. I could make it this evening … or whenever you're free.'

We met at 7pm at The Red Lion.

If Czech life revolves around drinking *(to be discussed)* The Red Lion must be the fulcrum of Czech civilization. It's a wonderful place, steeped in five hundred years of plots, conspiracies and revolutionary movements all doomed, in the Czech way, to be extinguished by a bit of defenestration or decapitation. As a pub, it's a classic. You have to get there early.

We did, and were given a small table in a corner, underneath an array of barrels, banners and cobwebs. It was Pilsner Urquell. Not my personal favourite, but the gold standard of Czech beer nonetheless.

'I'm so pleased you could spare me the time, Mr McKerrell.'

He was older than I'd expected, thinning hair but bushy grey eyebrows. He had a military air about him. A pleasant, square face. Dark eyes. I felt I could trust him – but I was on

Heroes

my guard because *'Vauxhall'* and its enemies specialized in recruiting people just like Mr DeVere.

'I expect you want some ID.'

'Yes please' I said, expecting him to produce a document.

'OK. Fabian, Adrian, McCoig. Tabor. *Here's tae us, an' wha's like us.*'

This was clever. If he was the opposition, he was too clever for me.

Then he said:

'You could ring Alasdair. He knows me.'

I did. I pointed my phone at DeVere and said: 'Kosher?'

Alasdair laughed. 'Yes, but he's Presbyterian.'

Safe ground, it seemed. We raised our glasses.

'So, Mr DeVere …'

'David, please. And may I call you Ian?'

'Of course. I'm very pleased to meet you. But what's it all about?'

'I want to talk to you about Sir Reginald.'

'Sir Reginald? Me? Why? I hardly know the man.'

'That's the point.'

'But … but … I'm not *supposed* to know him. He's God and I'm a minor earthling'. Why would anyone want to talk to me about Sir Reginald? Unless … they were a very devious covert operator for the other side …'

I stared at him narrowly.

'I wish it were always like this. Fair play to you. You're quite right to be careful. If only everyone was.' A faraway look came into his eyes.

'OK. You're not Guy Burgess and you're not Karla. But you seem to know who I am, for some reason. Now, what's it all about?'

'I have a strange job, Ian. I believe Sir Reginald intimated that the Department had…plans for you. I hope that's not indiscreet.'

'He may have done. Whoever he is.'

'Goodness … I really wish more of them were like you. But let me plunge on. My job – a strange one, as I have mentioned – is somewhere between training, indoctrination and briefing… in short, to give the Department's key people …'

He looked me straight in the eye.

' … a bit of background, so to speak. Do I make myself clear?'

'No, but keep talking. I will keep drinking.'

DeVere actually laughed.

'All right! All right! I'll get to the point. I'm here to tell you something about the history of the Department, and Sir Reginald's role in it, that you won't find in any book, and never will.'

I sat back. This could be interesting. And I didn't have to say anything.

'Everyone calls him God.'

I raised an eyebrow in assent.

'Well, he wasn't always God. Obviously. This is the point, really. Young men like yourself…'

All at once I liked him a lot more.

'Young men like yourself won't know anything about Sir Reginald – or plain Handiside, as he then was – when he 'won his spurs', so to speak. It's not on the record, so I'm here to fill the gap, as it were.'

I realised this was going to be a long seminar, so I drained my glass. Sure enough another arrived in thirty seconds.

'Please cast your mind back to the early years of World War Two.'

Heroes

I couldn't, having been born twenty-four years after it ended. But I'd been devouring books about it since I learnt to read. I hoped this was what he meant.

'In 1940 we had no idea what the Germans were up to because we had no agents- not a single one – in Nazi-occupied territory.'

He stared at me. Did he expect me to look shocked? I wasn't. I knew all about the timid UK government in office until May that year, and so had the Germans. We'd got no agents because, just like Josef Stalin, we were praying that Hitler meant what he said when he claimed to want peace.

'We needed to act quickly. Cutting a long story short, a group of Dutch speakers were smuggled into the Netherlands, some by ship and some by parachute. Their mission was to cross the border and make their way into Germany.'

He paused dramatically.

'All but two were apprehended at the border and … shot.'

I knew this but I put on the correct shocked expression.

'One made his way back to England. Captain Butterworth. Dead now, of course.

I looked interested.

'The other was Kenneth Handiside. He managed to evade the dragnet, make his way to Erfurt and sent us priceless information for the next two years.'

I was meant to look surprised, and I was. I hadn't read about this.

'You won't have read about this. It's all still buried in the archives with a 100-year label. There's a good reason for that.'

'What?'

'Because Handiside then contrived – no-one knows how – to get himself into the Soviet Union, where he did exactly the same thing for the next fifteen years.'

Heroes

My jaw hung open. This was truly astonishing. The fact that it had been done was incredible enough, but *how* had it been done? How on earth did a twenty-year-old stripling get himself accepted as persona grata by the ultra-suspicious Russians? It was beyond my imagination. They shot their own people on a whisper, let alone foreigners.

Was it true? I only had DeVere's word for it. But if it wasn't true, why was he bothering? It made no difference to the Department whether I thought Sir Reginald's father was a hero or knew nothing about either of them.

'I hope this is useful. I'm trying to paint a portrait of the Department's unsung history. It's a bit like a good regiment ... fathers and sons, family connections ...'

This made sense. The 'business' was all about trust. Hence the shock, horror and cover-ups when it turned out that four (or five) of the Department's most-trusted senior people had been laughing up their sleeves for years.

There was more, of course. We drank five half-litres each. He had a lot to say and I was a receptive audience. When he seemed to be running out of steam I made the traditional suggestion.

'Well, now. Shall we finish off the evening with a good malt?'

DeVere was taken aback.

'Oh – no – I don't think so, thank you. I've had quite enough, and anyway I never mix my drinks.'

This was the moment when he lost my confidence. Had he been spinning me a web of lies.?

But if so, why? What possible reason could there be for DeVere to come all the way to Prague and tell me a fabricated legend about Sir Reginald Handiside and his revered dad? *If* that's what it was. I was confused, but I knew the Department specialized in what is nowadays called 'story-telling'. If this was a 'story', why *him* and why *me*?

Anyway, the malt-test had sunk my visitor. I was puzzled and curious. There must be more to this than met the naked eye.

An awful idea came to mind. M15 knew there'd been a Fifth Man in the Cambridge spy-ring, but they never pinned him down. Rumours circulated for years about someone very senior – Sir Roger Hollis was often mentioned – being a long-term, deep-cover Soviet agent at the very top of the British intelligence establishment.

What if … no, it couldn't be true. But I had to speculate. *What if* the mole at the top had been Sir Reginald all this time? *What if* Kenneth Handiside and his son had been running a very different kind of family business? It didn't bear thinking about.

I began to speculate that the meeting with DeVere could have been a sales-pitch after all.

If so, no sale.

But I'd soon have chance to find out.

Galena's Preview

A posh envelope was delivered to the door. This was an event in itself: the only physical mail I received these days was a monthly statement of charges from my bank in Scotland.

We opened it when I got home. It contained an invitation from Galena to her new exhibition – 'Those Who Seek Asylum'. The topic was no surprise but the invitation was. Had I made it at last onto the list of Prague's movers and shakers? No, it couldn't be that. More likely Galena was scratching around to fill up her gallery on preview night.

The invitation was a work of art. It was a hologram. Czechs and Slovaks were good at this kind of thing. To my mind this was a national talent overshadowed by heavy engineering, weapons and cars.

I could think of twenty reasons not to go. But Petra could think of one reason why we should: she wanted to. So, with a happy smile matching hers, I accepted with pleasure.

'What am I going to wear?'

'Last time I went to one of these things everyone was in black' I said helpfully.

'Oh, Ian, please keep up! Black is *so* last-year! No, it's got to be red – but not just *red*, if you see what I mean, but something in that general area of the spectrum … subtle, nuanced, unusual …'

'I wish I could help, but to me a peony is the same as a traffic-light.'

The thought of seeking my help hadn't crossed her mind.

'I'll ask Andrew. He's *exactly* the right person to take on a trip to Parizska. Oh, I can't wait! This is so exciting!' She picked up her phone.

Galena's Preview

It was a long conversation. I imagined the pair of them coming back laden with carrier-bags from Prague's most expensive shops.

Which is exactly what happened.

We arrived at Male namesti on time, fifteen minutes late, and found ourselves queuing on a red carpet behind Alasdair and Andrew, who definitely *were* on the list of Prague's movers and shakers.

'Petra, you look absolutely wonderful!'

It was true. She did. I was proud.

We went in. The usual subdued lighting. It took a few minutes to adjust.

When I looked round at the exhibits, they seemed to be much the same as I'd seen at Galena's previous show. Miserable people, gaunt and hopeless. No soft-focus, everything portrayed in stark contrast, monochrome.

It was effective. You could have opinions about asylum policy, and it seemed to me that everyone did. But you couldn't have an *opinion* about human beings at the end of their tether. These images struck at a level where thinking, ideas and policies didn't really come into it. We were seeing men, women and children who were helpless.

I was lost in thought when someone grabbed my arm.

'*Ian!* I am so pleased you could make it! Welcome to the gallery!'

Galena, pretending that we were the best of friends.

'I am hearing such good things about Lanark! And, as you can see, things are not so bad with the gallery!'

I felt pleased that Galena was cheerful and evidently successful.

'You've done something extraordinary, Galena,' I said. 'You've touched the social consciences of all these rich people through the medium of art. If I hadn't seen it I would never have thought it possible.'

She gave me a quick look. Did I mean it? Yes, I did.

'Now, I am going to take you away and introduce you to some old friends!'

She hauled me through the crowd like a tug-boat.

'Stepan! Katerina! You remember Ian!'

It was him.

We shook hands. Then I shook hands with his daughter.

She spoke first. 'So, Mr McKerrell, have you been moved by the awful plight of these refugees shown here? ... Such powerful imagery ...'

'Yes, indeed, pani Sokolova. I have rarely seen an exhibition which made such a strong impression on me.'

I needed to say something to her father, but I was still numb.

Hackworth had killed him! The Department had celebrated the success of the 'operation'! Yet here he was, alive and well, drinking champagne.

I had to pretend that everything was normal. I turned to him.

'And has the exhibition affected your own feelings, pane Sokol?'

'Yes, it has. But I can only say that it has done nothing more than increase my own sympathy for the plight of innocent victims who are forced to flee and hope for better opportunities in other countries.'

He gave me the same level, blue-eyed, innocent look that I remembered from our first meeting. I felt chilled. Was he a psychopath? But Sokol was entirely at ease.

Galena's Preview

'Your own country has, I believe, some difficulty in agreeing on a policy for the management, so to say, of cross-channel asylum-seekers?'

'My own country, pane Sokol, is Scotland. We are not an attractive destination for migrants – at least, not since the Vikings. '

'Yes indeed, Mr McKerrell. I understand. One of our companies has a small property in Dumfries. But I expect you know this.'

He gave me that level, blue-eyed look again.

'I didn't know that, pane Sokol. I know nothing about you, though I obviously know that Katerina is the best horsewoman in Central Europe. That's public knowledge.'

He looked at me, at his daughter, at Galena, then around the room at the other guests. Then at me again.

This time I caught a hint of steel in his eyes.

'Knowledge. What do we really know? How do we know what we think we know? Are we facing unknown unknowns, as Donald Rumsfeld warned us? Please be aware of these issues, Mr McKerrell.'

Alasdair and Andrew swept us off for dinner at Zatisi. My mind was in a whirl. The 'operation' had failed. Who should I tell? Heads would roll, and I didn't want mine to be one of them.

Sokol was alive and well, and confident enough to issue me with a veiled threat. What was really going on? Hackworth, for all his apparent savoir-faire, had screwed up. Who had he really killed in Sokol's lake? Why had the Department celebrated a successful conclusion to the operation?

I wondered if I should tell Fabian, but then – what if Fabian had been complicit in Hackworth's failure? Who could be trusted? These were people who'd protected Philby for years

Galena's Preview

while he was systematically condemning their colleagues to a shot in the back of the neck from a Makarov PM. Who could I rely on? No-one.

I decided to go straight to the top. Phone or email? No, I would have to deliver this unwelcome news in person.

Face-to-Face with God

The taxi dropped me at New Covent Garden and I walked up to Vauxhall Cross. They were expecting me, so the check-in ritual only took twenty minutes. At last a guard collected me and took me up to the tenth floor.

I was ushered into the presence.

'Ian! How nice to see you again! How are things in the land of beer and boobs, eh?'

'Generally fine, Sir, but there's something I need to tell you. I think it's important. I am sorry to take up your time like this, but I didn't know who else to speak to.'

Sir Reginald gave the same grey-haired impression of someone who had seen everything a hundred times and could be surprised by nothing.

'Well, Ian, what exactly is it that made you jump on a plane and come all this way in person?'

'To put it bluntly, Sir: Stepan Sokol is *not dead*.'

'And ...?

'Umm – well – er - after the Tabor operation and the celebration – you know, when we all congratulated ourselves, in this very room – I thought... you ought to know ... that ... Sokol was still alive ... and ... well, I just thought I should tell you.'

Sir Reginald looked at me and may have smiled. It was hard to know.

'Ian.. let me offer you a drink.'

It was not an offer.

He poured out glasses of Aberlour 16.

'This should suit a Lowlander like you!'

We drank.

'Ian. How can I put this? Things are not always as they seem in the world of – what do we call it these days? – secret intelligence. I do not want to embarrass you with information you shouldn't have. Indeed, I cannot. Even so, I sense that you are a decent chap, so I want to confirm that *everything that has happened*, and *everything you have done*, is exactly in line with HMG's policy.'

I must have looked mystified.

Sir Reginald sighed. He took another sip of Aberlour.

'I am not explaining because I need to. I don't. I would prefer not to. But, by pure chance, you have stumbled upon something that needs clarifying. Why does it need clarifying, you might ask.'

Was I meant to answer? I said nothing, which turned out to be correct.

'There is a reason why, most unusually, I intend to introduce you – in this instance – to the 'bigger picture', as I believe it's called.'

He glared at me. I kept silent, which was the right thing to do.

'Simply put, we have plans for you, young man.'

He had my full attention. I wasn't used to be called 'young' and I liked it.

'Stepan Sokol, who, as you know, is – to speak plainly – a piece of utter shit – is, *nevertheless*, useful to HMG from time to time and in certain circumstances. He is in a position to supply munitions to people who, in the view of our lords and masters, need them and should have them. Are you with me so far?'

'I think so.'

Face-to-Face with God

'Good. However … our best friends on the other side of the Atlantic can occasionally take a slightly different view. It's not necessarily their fault…'

He sniffed and took another drink.

'They have their ways, we have ours … it's not worth going into … but the result can be … do you see where I'm going with this?'

I wasn't always slow.

'Yes, Sir. I think so. Our allies had to think that we'd retired Sokol while *really* we left him alive to continue doing things that we, the British, want him to do?'

He poured another glass.

'Pretty much spot-on. Normally, chaps on the front line don't need to know this kind of thing. It can be dangerous for them. And for us. But in this particular case I feel obliged to bring you, so to speak, on side.'

'I am grateful, Sir Reginald.'

Then he bowled a googly.

'Let me ask you … strictly between ourselves … what is your opinion of Adrian Hackworth?'

I didn't know what I was supposed to say, so I waffled.

'I never got to know him very well, Sir Reginald… but as far as I could tell he is a very competent member of that particular section of the Department's staff…'

Sir Reginald gave me a look. I quailed.

'Ian, you're no fool and neither am I. Now: what do you *really* think of Adrian Hackworth?'

'If I have to be candid, Sir Reginald… I thought he was a bit too talkative. Indiscreet. I couldn't understand why someone that that would be employed by the Department.'

Had I spoken out of turn? Was this the end of my time with SIS?

Face-to-Face with God

But Handiside just stared at me. He may have frowned and he may have smiled. I couldn't tell. Time passed.

'Have you heard the expression 'useful idiots'? Well, we have them too.'

I thought about this.

'Ah!' I said at last.

Sir Reginald definitely smiled this time and poured another glass. We drank.

The meeting was at an end.

Should I, could I, would I? I had to.

'Sir Reginald, may I ask you something rather personal?'

He looked surprised. This wasn't what junior staff did at The Presence.

But he was a *gentleman* and knew what to say.

'Of course, dear boy. Fire away.'

'Sir Reginald ... do you know the identity of the Fifth Man?'

He looked straight at me. For a moment I thought I saw fear, maybe anger. But his eyes were expressionless and somehow vacant. It was as if I was looking right through him.

Then he smiled again. That same world-weary grimace, half-hidden behind the beard and the moustache. But there was no smile in his eyes.

'Hah! I wish I had a pound for every time I've been asked that question.'

He looked away and seemed lost in thought. Then he looked back at me.

'McKerrell, I'm far too old to care. And you're far too young for anyone to pay attention to you. Do you want my advice?'

I stammered 'Yes, Sir.'

'Just get on with your job.'

Face-to-Face with God

I thought I had my answer. DeVere and Butterworth had been sent to allay a suspicion which hadn't existed before they spoke to me. Now I thought I knew the truth. But what difference did it make? He was right. There was nothing I could do. There was no 'higher cause' here. My only option was to get on with the job.

Fabian called me on a clear line two weeks later.

'I'm afraid I've got some rather distressing news to impart. I am very sorry to have to tell you – *very* sorry indeed – that Adrian Hackworth was killed in a motor accident on the A3 yesterday.'

'Oh dear. That's sad. How did it happen?'

'We're not quite sure yet. It looks as if he was having a race and lost control of his MX-5. But I know the two of you were close, so I felt I ought to give you the news personally.'

Close? Hackworth? Me? Where on earth did Fabian get that idea?

'That's very good of you, Fabian. But in all honesty, I barely knew Hackworth – I only met him twice, once here and once in London.'

'That's odd. He was forever singing your praises in the Department. We all got the impression you were his 'best mate', as I believe the vernacular has it. Hmm?'

This made me think. Hackworth, half schoolboy and half ghoul. Was he really so lonely that a bloke who'd bought him a pint and taken him to Barrandov had become his BFF?

Apparently so. What a waste. It was ironic. Someone who'd spent his career courting danger had snuffed himself out by accident, playing boy-racer games in Surrey. Or so Fabian was telling me.

I resolved to light a candle for Hackworth at the Church of the Holy Nativity.

Andelska Hora

I heard the sound of a Spitfire approaching fast and roaring overhead. It was my phone. It meant unknown number.

'Hello?'

'Hello – is that Ian?'

I knew at once it was Katerina Sokol. Did she want another trip to Barrandov?

'I'm calling on behalf of my father. He wants to meet you.'

Two questions. What for? And why couldn't he call me himself? But I didn't ask.

'OK, Katerina. Where and when?'

'He wonders if you could be so kind as to meet him at the castle at Andelska Hora. And would tonight at 10 pm be convenient?'

Peculiar. Ominous. Maybe dangerous. Or was it just that dodgy arms dealers felt obliged to shroud everything they did in mystery?

Or had he found out about my role in his intended assassination and wanted to square accounts somewhere remote?

'Katerina… it seems a long way to go for a chat. Could I suggest the bar at the Hotel Savoy instead?'

'He is very sorry if it is a nuisance, Ian. But I know he uses the ruin quite often to meet his contacts … it's not far from Karlovy Vary.'

This could be true. Karlovy Vary was a favourite Russian haunt.

I wondered what to say. What would James Bond say?. I knew the answer, but I wasn't James Bond. Then: hang on a minute! If you're going to be 'operational' you'd better *be* operational!

Andelska Hora

'OK, Katerina, please tell you father I'll be there at 10 pm. But it's a big place … how will we meet up?'

'Do you know how to hoot like an owl?'

'Yes, I do, as a matter of fact.'

'Wonderful. He will give one hoot and you will give two hoots. Then you will find each other.'

Should I explain what 'two hoots' meant in English? No, life was too short.

'Very good, Katerina. Your wish is my command.'

She giggled and ended the call.

I made one.

'Alasdair? Are you busy this evening?'

'Yes. I'm teaching Andrew fusion. Chateaubriand with neeps and tatties.'

'Could I ask you a massive favour?'

'It'll cost you.'

'Anything!'

I told Alasdair about my rendez-vous with Sokol at a ruined castle in the middle of nowhere. He laughed.

'So I suppose you want me there to provide close protection?'

'Exactly! Are you up for it?'

'Of course. All in a day's work for Stirling Security.'

'Thank you, thank you.'

'You haven't heard the price.'

'Whatever! Just name it!'

'Are you sure you want to hear this?'

'Yes!'.

'There are three parts to the price.'

'Yes, yes. What?'

Andelska Hora

'All right … let me think, now …. first, you have to swear that William Wallace was a true Scots patriot, the bravest of the brave.'

'Agreed'.

'In front of witnesses.'

'Yes.'

'Notarized.'

'Agreed.'

'Second … you have to sign a document stating that you abandon all allegiance to Hearts – you never really liked them – and you'll attend every Hibs home fixture for a year …'

'Yes, yes. OK!'

'… I haven't finished. Sitting in the South Stand and cheering for the home team!'

I wanted Alasdair to protect my personal safety. But here he was, cheerfully condemning me to death.

'OK. OK. Agreed. Is that it?'

'No, no, no. I said *three*. Let me see, now. Ah – I've got it. You have to eat a whole haggis in front of Andrew, Petra and me. No water.'

'Ugh. Yes, OK.'

'500 grammes.'

Aaarrgghh.

I realised why Alasdair looked half as old as his chronological age. The man was a big kid. Life was a party, everything was a game. His price consisted of forfeits.

'Yes! I'll do it! Are you on?'

'Of course. I said so. Pick me up at five o'clock.'

'But it only takes two hours.'

I heard Alasdair sigh.

'Ian… just do what I say. You're new to this game. *He* will get there early, so *we'll* get there earlier. Recce – positions –

Andelska Hora

ready. *He* won't see me. But *I'll* know if he's alone or … something else.'

I picked Alasdair up at 5pm on the dot. He was wearing black from head to foot and carrying a long case which looked as if it contained a bassoon.

'Are you going to play us the Mozart concerto in B-flat major?'

He gave me a pitying glance. There were obviously some jokes too childish even for Alasdair.

Out of Prague and onto the E48. 120 kph, legal speed.

The terrain here was flat, all the way to the German border, punctuated every so often by the remains of extinct volcanoes. They poked up, bare and rocky, like the Devil's Tower in 'Close Encounters'. William once told me why and how, but I'd forgotten. Nearly every one of them had a ruined castle on top.

We turned off and headed for the village of Andelska hora. 'Angel's Hill'. I wondered why these magma buttes were attributed to heaven in Bohemia and hell in Wyoming. We drove up a tree-covered slope.

'Stop here.'

'Why here?'

'Because we need to hide the car. Duh! He's not supposed to know we got here before him.'

I followed his instructions and parked inside a stand of hornbeams. We got out and Alasdair opened his case. He produced a two-metre sculpture of steel and wood with a hole in the stock.

'Dragunov SVD. Best sniper rifle ever made. I tell you, Ian, when the Russians really put their minds to it, they're fantastic. T-34, Sputnik, RD-180 rocket engines … nothing to beat them.'

Andelska Hora

'Yes. An excellent weapon.'

'How would *you* know?'

I could have told him but I wanted to keep Alasdair happy. 'Just what I've read'.

We began walking.

'What now, Ali? Are we doing our 'recce'?'

'Done, old son. Google Earth and Sentinel. I will be up *there…*'

He pointed to a ruined tower with a commanding view.

'And you will be here … he pointed to a nearby rock.'

'And then?' I asked humbly.

'*Then* we wait for full darkness and Mr Sokol. I'll watch every move he makes. If I suspect anything's amiss … well, Drago and I will make sure that nothing untoward happens.'

He gave me a cheerful smile, pulled a balaklava down over his face and set off. I lost sight of him in twenty seconds.

I looked around. Over there, a forest. On the other side, a range of low mountains. Down there, the village, with fields and farms beyond as far as the eye could see. The perfect site for a warlord's stronghold. I looked up at the ruins.

The castle must once have been magnificent, intimidating. It was still awe-inspiring. Massive stone blocks piled on top of each other, reaching up to dizzying heights. The whole monstrous edifice said *indestructible*. 'See me and tremble!' Whoever lived here was lord and master of all he surveyed. Safe, secure, free to extort his wealth from the peasants down below, free to rampage across his neighbours' lands.

It didn't last. One day someone came to Andelska hora – probably the Swedes, before they discovered neutrality – and burnt it out. Since then the ruins had been deserted, a favourite spot for hikers and families having picnics on sunny days. At night, a haven for bats and foxes.

Andelska Hora

And for arms-dealers holding private conversations with local representatives of the Department. Or so I hoped. If it was more, or less, than Katerina had said … well, I had my insurance policy.

After three cigarettes I found out.

'Hoot'.

'Hoot, hoot.'

A figure emerged from the murk and came towards me. When he got close I recognized Sokol. He paused and held out his hand. I shook it.

'I must thank you, Mr McKerrell, for neglecting the charming Petra – as I believe you call her – in favour of a nocturnal meeting with a boring old man like me.'

'Think nothing of it, pane Sokol. You yourself could have been buying horses with your exceptionally delightful daughter, but instead you have chosen to meet a lighting technician of no possible importance at a picturesque but distant ruin in Western Bohemia.'

Two could play at that game.

I think he smiled. At least, I saw his teeth.

'I expect you are wondering why we are here?'

'It had crossed my mind. But Katerina is a persuasive person, as I'm sure you know.'

I couldn't see his teeth any more.

'Mr McKerrell … I know a lot about you. I think I know everything that matters.'

'You are going into film production?'

'Come now, Mr McKerrell. Let's not waste time. I am referring – obviously – to your *other* role in life – primary, secondary, who knows? – the role connected with a certain garish building on the south bank of the River Thames.'

Andelska Hora

'I've seen it, pane Sokol, and I couldn't agree more with your adjective. We are not alone! Almost every architectural critic in Britain has condemned the crass modernity of its design. Why, only last month the *Architectural Review* …'

'Stop it! Please! I have no time for this English prevarication! And nor do you!'

I was pleased with myself. He seemed rattled. *Rule One* in confrontations: stay calm and push your opponent out of his comfort-zone. Now Sokol would have to get to the point.

'I must get to the point, Mr McKerrell. Time is short.'

'Please do.' *Cool, calm, collected.*

I couldn't see Sokol clearly, but I sensed that he was angry.

'There's something I need to know, Mr McKerrell.'

'And what might that be?'

'Simply this. I believe you are aware of the … relationship … which exists between my companies and certain people on the south bank of the River Thames?'

'Not really. Is there one?'

Now he was really angry, and didn't try to hide it.

'I was told you had been told! What the hell are these idiots in London paid for?'

'Please, pane Sokol. I have often wondered exactly the same thing.'

'Right. Right. Let me get to the point. I want to know – I need to know – if you intend to work within the existing system or – for whatever reason – disrupt a well-established *modus operandi*.'

It was a difficult question. I didn't know what the '*modus operandi*' was and moreover I didn't imagine for a minute that my new, 'operational role' with the Department could pose any kind of threat to Sokol.

But he did. This was interesting.

Andelska Hora

'I hear what you say, pane Sokol, and I'm not sure how to answer. On the one hand, it would obviously be my duty to conduct myself here in the Czech Republic exactly in accordance with my instructions ... were we to imagine, absurd though it is, that I occupy the position that you seem to imagine I do. On the other hand - and again, purely hypothetically - I think you might be asking me if I would be happy, in a personal sense, to continue working with a scumbag like yourself. Am I close?'

I couldn't see his face but he ducked his head and waved his right arm.

All at once, two shots rang out. This cliché doesn't do justice to what actually happened. The air was split by two very loud '*cracks*' which stunned me and made my ears ring. I was aware of two flashes but my eyes were blind. I saw nothing for thirty seconds. But my ears worked. I heard clumping sounds as though two large objects had crashed to the earth from a height.

As it turned out, this was exactly what had taken place. Sokol's gunmen were ready to kill me if I didn't give the answer their boss wanted. Alasdair spotted them and took them out when he saw Sokol raise his hand.

Sokol stared at me. Then, for the first time, he gave a genuine smile.

'Do you play chess, Mr McKerrell?'

'Not very well.'

'Not very well? You surprise me. I would say that you have put me in check this evening. I didn't see it coming. I should have done. Ah well… there is always something to learn.'

I said nothing, resolving to applaud William Wallace, abjure Hearts and eat a ton of haggis. My nutty friend had saved my life. Not only that, he'd also given me a temporary advantage over Sokol, and Sokol knew it.

He nodded and turned away, disappearing into the rocks and trees.

A minute later Alasdair bounded up.

'Not bad, eh? Two head-shots at 300 metres! Come on, now – is that world-class or is that world-class?'

I drove back to Prague at 120 kph. We went to the Black Lion and drank 'pints' and shots until closing time. Alasdair was like a dog with two tails. After our third 'pint' and chaser he said:

'You know all that stuff I said about William Wallace?'

'Yes.'

'I'm going to hold you to it.'

'I expected nothing less.'

'And you know what I said about the 500 gramme haggis?'

'Yes'.

'I'm holding you to that, too. It'll be such fun!'

'Yes, I agreed to do it and I will do it.'

'And you remember what I said about Hearts and Hibs? Sitting in the South Stand for a year? Cheering for the opposition – your own team?

'Of course I remember!'

'Well… I've been thinking… forget about it. I couldn't do that to a human being. Not even you.'

Trevor Toll

Fabian rang.

'All well, I hope? Petra well? Beaujolais well? Business going well? Hmm?'

I wasn't sure what to make of this new, affable Fabian. I preferred the old, supercilious version – it seemed more genuine.

'Everything's fine, thank you, Fabian. What can I do for you?'

'Good, good. That's good to hear. And Prague? All good? How's the weather there? A bit warmer now, I expect.'

I wondered when he would come to the point.

'I'd better come to the point. The Department – that is to say, my senior colleagues and I – those that are more or less directly concerned with affairs in *your part of the world* – would like to ask you to undertake a small mission, so to speak, which involves no risk or hazards this time – absolutely none, you'll be glad to hear – but which could have significant consequences for, what can I say … certain aspects of our operations in *your part of the world*.'

It wasn't 'my part of the world'. That was Lanarkshire. I wondered why he kept saying it. With Fabian it was impossible to know and pointless to speculate.

'Yes, Fabian. Happy to be of service.'

'Good, good. Very good. Good attitude, Ian. Very much in the best traditions of the Department, if I may say so.'

'Thank you, Fabian. But what *is* it?'

'Ah. I knew you'd be wondering. Well… you are, of course, aware of a certain businessman, quite important in *your part of the world* … whose initials are SS … hmm?'

If he meant Sokol this was a peculiar question. Fabian had sent me to take part in the failed attempt to assassinate Stepan Sokol at Tabor. He *must* have read my report on the assignation at Andelska Hora where Sokol narrowly failed to finish me off. Could he have forgotten?

'I knew we'd be on common ground. Good, good. Very good. Well… the gentleman in question is visiting London next week for an important meeting and … well, to cut to the chase, so to speak… we'd like you to accompany him. Hmm?'

This would be fun. I'd tried to drown him, he'd tried to shoot me, and now we'd be sitting next to each other on a plane. Why me, of all people?

'The gentleman in question has specifically asked for you. By name.'

'But why? He's got every reason to dislike me intensely!'

'Yes,' said Fabian. 'The same thought occurred to us, if I can say that without giving offence. I know it sounds strange, but apparently he trusts you. No idea why. Sorry – sorry, Ian – that must sound terrible. I do apologise. Not what I meant to say at all. Of course, he's got every reason in the world to trust you, just as we do. I hope I didn't inadvertently raise any hackles there… hmm?'

'No, Fabian. My hackles are on my socks. What do I have to do?'

Fabian explained that Sokol wanted to buy 45 'Acrobat' Infantry Fighting Vehicles manufactured by British Armoury Science PLC. There was a problem with the export licence because of questions about end-user verification. Sokol, and the Departmental sponsors of his 'Special Relationship' with SIS, thought the best solution was to engage a high-powered lobbyist. It would be deniable.

Trevor Toll

'Just a question of saying the right thing in the right ears ... and Bob's your uncle. Hmm?'

Could it really be as simple as that? I knew nothing of the obscure world of lobbying. I'd read about brown envelopes, questions in the House, massive fees paid under-the-counter, Ministers papped on Russian yachts. I knew it existed, but that was all. I said so.

'Fabian, what I know about lobbying would fill a thimble with room left over. What can someone like me possibly contribute?'

'Please don't worry, Ian. Or, as you might prefer - *dinna fash yourself*.'

I could tell that Fabian had covered the phone while he chortled at this shaft of rapier wit.

'The gentleman in question just needs friendly company in unfamiliar surroundings. Your role is quite straightforward. You are there to show that the Department has ... what can we call it ... an *interest* in a successful outcome. And who knows ... you may be able to act as an interpreter, if necessary ... being a fluent speaker of the English language – or should I say the *Scots* language?'

The phone was covered up again while Fabian got control of himself.

'English, Scots ... Czech ...it makes no difference.'

Fabian didn't know my Czech was limited to thirty words. He thought I was fluent.

We would be visiting Whitehall Consultants LLP and meeting Trevor Toll, founder, chairman, senior partner and top gun. To my surprise they weren't in Whitehall but in Brook Street, just opposite the Savile Club.

I expected a private jet. Sokol had two. But it was BA 853.

Trevor Toll

I met him at Vaclav Havel. Why were so many airports named after famous people these days? JFK, a dead 'Berliner'. George Best, a dead winger. John Lennon, a dead singer. I wondered how the Czech Republic's first president felt about the company he was keeping.

'Ah, Mr McKerrell. Very nice to see you again.' We shook hands. A large black SUV purred discreetly away.

We were in 1A and 1C. Of course. Sokol took the window. To my relief, he didn't seem inclined to talk and busied himself with his laptop.

At Heathrow my British passport meant I went straight through immigration while Sokol had to queue. I waited for him.

My usual habit was the Heathrow Express, but this wasn't Sokol's style. An even larger SUV was waiting for us outside the terminal. Ninety minutes later we were in Brook Street.

I looked sadly at the former American Embassy in Grosvenor Square. The eagle had long gone, and with it – I felt – much of the wartime 'special relationship' between the United States and the UK. The new US Embassy was on the South Bank, not far from the structure which Sokol had truthfully described as 'garish'.

A small brass plate identified Whitehall's offices. We went in.

Trevor Toll was waiting for us in reception between two enormous displays of flowers. Where was it Spring? Jersey, perhaps.

He strode forward with a beaming smile.

Toll was a big man. Tall, square, in good shape for a man of sixty. His hair was long and luxuriant. His face was wide and cheerful, exuding good health and friendliness. Blue eyes like Sokol's, but Toll's twinkled. He was regularly described as

Trevor Toll

'charismatic' and I could see why. We were enveloped in his charm before he said a word.

His clothes made a statement. The finest pin-striped fabric. Vicuna? Mohair? Silk tie, light blue (yes, he'd been at Cambridge). Discreet gold cuff-links. The statement was: I'm rich, successful and very well-connected. I can do whatever you need, but you'd better have plenty of money.

Sokol, of course, did.

Toll led us into his office on the ground floor, where a smartly-dressed young aide, looking very like Katerina Sokol, asked us what we'd like to drink. Sokol said water. I decided to make my own statement. 'Would you happen to have a Glenlivet?' They did, of course.

There was a partners' desk in the window-bay but Toll joined us at a low table in the middle of the room. While the aide served our drinks I looked around. A full-length portrait of the Duke of Wellington. Probably original. Another of Napoleon on a horse. A framed photograph of Tony Blair: 'To my dear friend Trevor…'. There was a clear message on the walls of Toll's office.

'Now, gentlemen', he said. 'I wonder if I could start by summarizing my understanding of the problem afflicting you?' Sokol said yes.

'Someone, somewhere, wants to buy Acrobats. No idea why. We don't want them and *we* can't sell them. But you can.' He raised his eyebrows.

'Yes, Mr Toll. I can' said Sokol.

'Well, that sounds like a win for everyone concerned, doesn't it?' The eyebrows again.

'Yes, Mr Toll. Money for British Armoury, money for HMG and a modest commission for me.'

Trevor Toll

'Quite. But there's the minor issue of an end-user certificate standing in the way… is that right?'

'Yes, so it would seem.'

Sokol certainly didn't need an interpreter.

'Hmm. Red tape. Hate it. Let's see what we can do.'

Toll picked up his phone and pressed two buttons.

'Brian? Hi, it's Trevor. Do you have half a minute?'

Brian Nevison was the current Minister of Defence.

'Excellent. Now – I've got a very charming young man in my office from the Czech Republic ….'

Sokol actually blushed.

' … and he's put together a really marvellous deal which will take 45 useless Acrobats off our hands and deliver a handsome price to our friends at British Armoury …'

'Yes, I couldn't agree more. Trouble is, someone's being a bit sticky about end-user verification, so the deal's stalled.'

'Yes, Brian, I was hoping you'd say that. Well, you're best-placed to un-stall it and put a smile on everyone's face, as you well know.'

'Fantastic! Thank you so much! Love to Martha!'

Toll stood up.

'Mr Sokol, I think you'll find that all the necessary documentation arrives at Czexport within the next few days.' He beamed at us.

We stood up, shook hands and were ushered out. I hadn't even finished my Glenlivet.

So *this* was lobbying.

It had been quick. Sokol's driver was in a café somewhere. Sokol rang him.

We had time on our hands. I made a suggestion.

'Pane Sokol … there's an extremely good Polish restaurant on our way back to the airport. I wonder if you feel like a snack?'

He frowned at the word 'Polish', but seemed to like the idea of *pierogi*, or perhaps *kielbasa*. I knew what I wanted: ice-cold bison-grass vodka, and plenty of it.

Twenty minutes later we went up the steps into Ognisko and were welcomed like old friends. We started in the bar. I would have been happy to stay there, but Sokol, a true Czech, had an appetite.

One of the many things I liked about Czechs was that they didn't feel the need to make polite conversation. They could sit contentedly for hours with hardly a word spoken. Sokol was no exception.

When we'd finished I asked him about Katerina and her chances at Badminton. Sokol confided that he'd be back in England for next month's sales at Tattersalls.

'But she said Kapitan was the best horse she'd ever owned!'

Sokol shrugged. 'Yes. But he's a horse. He won't last for ever.'

I heard Sokol's phone buzz. He picked it up and looked at the message.

'Sakra!'

'What's wrong?'

He didn't answer, just showed me his phone.

An invoice had arrived from Whitehall Consultants LLP.

'To: consultancy services in connection with Acrobat export licence: € 64,000-00. Terms: 30 days net.'

'Proboha zivyho!' Sokol was not happy.

What could I do? Nothing, really. I didn't care how much this creep had to pay a British lobbyist to get his deal approved. The more the better.

But I was the Department's representative. I had to make an effort.

'Pane Sokol. May I tell you a story about Louis XIV?'

'Why not.'

'The king suffered from poor health. He called in a doctor who diagnosed the problem, prescribed a course of treatment and was gone from the palace in 30 minutes. The cure worked. The king then received a bill for 100,000 livres. He summoned the doctor.'

'This is outrageous! 100,000 livres for half an hour's work? Are you mad?'

'No, Sire. Let me explain. The bill is actually 100 livres for thirty minutes attending Your Majesty and 99,900 livres for forty years' experience enabling your humble servant to arrive at an effective remedy.'

'They say the King shrugged and handed over the money without demur.'

For the second time since I'd met him, Sokol smiled. His face returned to its normal colour and our journey home was peaceful.

I felt I had upheld the best traditions of the Department.

Sarka Valley

There is very little public nudity in Lanarkshire. I don't know why. Calvinism, conformity, climate? Our knowledge of female anatomy came from Malcolm's dad's secret stash of 'Health & Efficiency'. Until we were thirteen and Deirdre entered our lives.

Not so in the Czech Republic. In many ways shy and private souls, the Czechs get their kit off at the drop of a hat.

It was the first really sunny day of the year and Petra's hat was ready to drop. 'Let's snatch some rays!'

Dogs weren't allowed, so Beaujolais stayed in with double Winalot.

We crossed the bridge and caught a number 20 tram to the Sarka Valley. This wilderness of towering limestone crags and meandering streams is just on the edge of the city. It took twenty minutes.

We followed a steep pathway to the valley floor. On either side maples and ashes were in bud. Down in the gorge there was no wind at all and the sun was hot. We took a branching path to Dzban, our destination. It's a spring-fed reservoir which the city has turned into a bathing-area in the middle of a nature-reserve.

I remembered my last visit to a lake and shuddered. Petra could see the water and lengthened her stride.

Dzban offers two bathing options: 'textile' and 'naturist'. I went in the wrong direction.

'Come on, Ian!' yelled Petra. *'This way!'*

We were going to take all our clothes off. In Petra's case, this was a marvellous idea. In my case, less so.

Petra marched across the grass until she found the perfect spot. It was a goldilocks zone: not too near other people

Sarka Valley

(weird) and not too distant (weird). There were plenty of people about but the grass stretched as far as the eye could see. We spread our towels.

'Come on, Ian! Let's go swimming!'

'I think I'll just … acclimatize for a few minutes, if you don't mind.'

'Oh, Ian! Don't be such a loofah!'

In the blink of an eye Petra was stark naked and running towards the water's edge. She dived straight in and began slicing through the water like Katie Ledecky.

I wanted to warm up before joining her. I sat on my towel and cautiously removed my clothes. I suppose I was worried about people watching me, but no-one was.

The sun beat down. There was no sound except occasional squeaks from excited children and the twitter of the birds. Peace and quiet. Time for my book. 'A Distant Mirror' by Barbara Tuchman.

I'd spent seven years at Lanark Grammar and learnt nothing. This disappointed both parents but they didn't agree on the diagnosis. 'He's too intelligent – bored stiff' said my dad. 'He's bone-idle' said my mam.

Either way, I'd now begun remedial education. My body was too far gone for Pencat Silat but my brain still worked. I started with medieval history because it would give me something to say to Father Dominic. It might also help in arguments with Alasdair.

I looked up from time to time to check on Petra. I could see a dot far out in the middle of the lake, ploughing up and down. Where did she get the energy? She ate like a bird but swam like a fish.

Sarka Valley

At length I decided to put down my book, gird my loins and set off for the water. I stood up, hesitantly. But no-one was looking.

Then I spotted something that would never have made the pages of 'Health & Efficiency'. Between me and the lake stood two young women locked in a passionate embrace. Their arms were wrapped round each other and they were kissing. I had to look. So did everyone else.

They were in profile. One had brown hair, the other blonde. Entwined, they would have graced the pages of any magazine that wanted to push the envelope. Vogue, for example. They were magnificent. They had captured the attention of a large audience and seemed unconcerned.

Then they disentangled themselves and turned towards me in their full, naked glory. For once the word was apposite.

'*Ian!*'

Cardiac arrest.

It was Katerina and Zuzana.

They walked towards me hand-in-hand.

Instinctively, I turned away. Peals of laughter.

'Ian McKerrell! What are you doing here?' said Katerina. 'And *what* are you hiding?'

'Ian… are you a clandestine voyeur?' said Zuzana, grinning. 'I *knew* you had a secret! Now I know what it is!'

I was speechless. *Help!*

At that very moment Petra bounded up, spraying water in all directions. She figured out the situation in two seconds.

Breathing deeply, she stood with arms akimbo. A Naiad. Sculptural, ravishing. Katerina and Zuzana observed her with keen interest.

'Ian – won't you introduce me to your friends?'

Sarka Valley

I did so, linking my hands modestly as a sporran. But I needn't have bothered. My 'friends' didn't spare me a look. They were examining Petra in forensic detail.

I was sent away to get refreshments from the café.

When I returned, Petra was sitting on her towel. Katerina and Zuzana were sitting on mine. They were deep in conversation.

I sat on the grass and listened.

'So, if a VIP you're guarding is threatened, you have to do … what, exactly? Immobilize them? Shoot them?'

'We hardly ever use firearms. That would be considered a failure. But yes… our job is to neutralise a threat by incapacitating the person in question.'

'Incredible! I couldn't do that in a million years!'

'Amazing! But *how*? What do you *actually do*?'

'I could describe it to you… but would you like a small demonstration?'

'*Oooh* … yes please!'

The three of them got up and made their way, without a backward glance, towards a copse of Alders.

I packed up my things and walked to the tram-stop.

I was out of my league in so many ways. I would have to do something.

Unarmed Combat

It's a beautiful day in Hampshire. I can hear plovers on the marshes. The grass is soft and springy beneath my feet. The sun is out and puffy clouds are drifting from the Solent across the horizon. All things considered, it's a perfect English day. But not quite.

In front of me is McCoig. He is now an instructor at Hambleside. He's been demoted, and he blames me.

I'm doing the Department's unarmed combat course. I have decided to go operational. Lanark Lighting is in Andrew's safe hands. We talk daily.

But right now I have other things to think about.

McCoig approaches me. His normal blank countenance is twisted into a sneer. He thinks it's my fault that Svetlana dumped him. He thinks it's my fault he was blue-flagged and given a job as an instructor. Now he wants to make me pay.

Before I know it I'm on my back and McCoig is kneeling on my throat. He emits a grunt. His face looks like a praying mantis.

I can't breathe. I can feel my eyes bulging and pressure building up in my head. But I can still think, and as McCoig leans harder I realise that he's not instructing me. He's trying to kill me.

At this moment I hear a voice some distance away. McCoig turns his head to look and I seize my chance.

I know about karate. At least, I think I do. Is it part of Krav Maga, or MMA, or something else? It doesn't matter. I swing the heel of my hand with all the force I can muster into the gap under McCoig's nose. He falls over and I can breathe again.

Unarmed Combat

Major Butterworth trots up. 'I say, you chaps ...' He's a portly man and slightly red in the face. 'Take it easy, will you? We're supposed to be *simulating* combat situations for instructional purposes.'

'Tell that to him', I reply, still coughing.

We both turn to look at McCoig. He isn't moving or, apparently, breathing.

'Good God!' says Butterworth. 'Look – I'll start with CPR and you can get going on mouth-to-mouth.'

'No.'

Butterworth glances at me. 'OK – I'll do mouth-to-mouth, you give him 100 compressions a minute. Use the rhythm of 'Stayin' Alive'.

'But Sir ... I can't stand the Bee Gees.'

'*Get on with it!*'

We get on with it. Butterworth sweats and gulps, I pant. Nothing happens. McCoig has shuffled off this mortal coil and it isn't shuffling back.

As expected. I'd used 'Fireball'. McCoig didn't stand a chance.

'Oh dear, oh dear' laments Butterworth. 'This has never happened at Hambleside. It's never happened. Never. There'll have to be an investigation ... a full report ... then a Board of Enquiry ... oh dear ...'

I do my best to look solemn. It would be 'a most unfortunate incident', 'an unanticipated freak occurrence'. Perhaps even 'a tragedy'.

But I knew better.

I was going to like this.

Unarmed Combat

Czech Glossary

Ahoj! Jak se mas?	*Hi! How are you?*
Anglicky – nemluvim cesky, prominte	*English – don't speak Czech – sorry*
Barrandov	*Prague film studios, largest in Europe*
Becherovka	*Popular liqueur made in Karlovy Vary*
Café Slavia	*Brasserie patronized by Vaclav Havel*
Cerna Hora	*Highly-regarded Moravian brewery*
Dobry den!	*Good day! Universal Czech greeting*
Dopravni policie	*Traffic police*
Kajetanka	*Up-market residential development*
Kava	*Coffee*
Kozel	*Popular beer from Velke Popovice*
Lida Baarova	*Actress, mistress of Goebbels*
Ma Vlast	*'My Country', symphony by Smetana*
Mala Strana	*Prague's Bohemian quarter*
Matryoshka	*Russian set of nested dolls*
Milacku	*Term of endearment – honey, darling*
Namesti	*Square*
Pane, pani	*Sir (Mr), Madame (Ms)*

Czech Glossary

Pariszka	*Prague's Bond Street*
Perekurushka	*Russian for smoke-break*
Pivovar	*Brewery*
Proboha zivyho!	******* *******!*
Puska	*Gun, rifle*
Semtex	*Czech explosive*
StB	*Communist secret police*
Tabor	*Historic town in South Bohemia*
Universita Karlova	*Charles University*
Vaclav Havel	*First President after independence*
Vltava	*River running through Prague*
Zatisi	*(v Zatisi) upmarket restaurant*
Zeny	*Ladies*

Printed in Great Britain
by Amazon